MURDER AT THE GRAND HOTEL

Isabella Bassett

CONTENTS

The French Riviera, 1925

CHAPTER 1

"Nice, two hours," the train conductor announced discreetly as he made his way through the dining carriage, as though not to disturb English sensibilities so early in the morning.

Exchanging a polite smile with him as he passed my table, I returned my attention to the view out the window. The scenery had changed overnight. Gone were the dreary skies of London, replaced by palm trees, wisterias climbing ancient stone walls, yellow ochre Italianate villas basking in the morning sun, and the blinding turquoise blue of the Mediterranean in the distance.

I marveled at the speed with which the train had conveyed us overnight to the South of France and gave a silent thanks to the enterprising company that had introduced this luxury service just three short years ago, in 1922.

"Now, my dear, as we discussed last night, your mother has written to me about your situation at length," said Lady Morton, currently sitting across from me at breakfast, and I turned my gaze back to her reluctantly.

ISABELLA BASSETT

Much to my regret, Lady Morton appeared to be a woman on a mission. Through a series of events in London, my perceived matrimonial value had decreased. She saw this as an opportunity to attach her Cecil to me. She was a shrewd woman and knew that under regular circumstances, her son was no match for me. But, as she considered my current situation to have reduced my stock on the wedding market, she calculated that now was the time to acquire a bride at a discount.

A large woman, displaying an ample bosom counterbalanced by a beaked nose, she looked as though she had expanded simply to take full advantage of the comforts fortune had granted her.

Her hat, buttressed by a voluminous pompadour, signaled to the casual bystander that this was a woman not to be trifled with. With fashion and morals thus safely anchored in the Victorian era, she bobbed unencumbered on the waters of the new century, free to intimidate all in her vicinity.

Using her impressive presence, Lady Morton had deterred anyone else from approaching me the entire trip, and I had been her captive audience since we embarked upon the Blue Train in Calais yesterday.

I looked around at my fellow passengers. Dressed in their holiday lights and whites, some even displaying Optimo Panamas and straw boating hats by their elbows, they all appeared delighted to have escaped the oppressive skies of England.

And although I myself was not going down to the Riviera on holiday, I was nevertheless just as delighted to be escaping London. I congratulated myself on thwarting my mother's latest efforts and narrowly avoiding a union with the most frightful bore of the golfing persuasion.

"Quite, right," Lady Morton continued, and I had to admit I had no idea what she was referring to. "Now, I have it in mind to write to Cecil to join us. He so enjoys a good game of tennis."

Oh, not a tennis bore.

Thus far, I had circumvented nuptial unions by educating myself to such a degree as to render me, I hoped, unmarriageable. First, I had convinced my mother to allow me to attend St. Hilda's at Oxford. Then, in exchange, I had agreed to spend a year at a finishing school in Switzerland, which, as luck would have it, had not been exactly what my mother had hoped for.

"Do not worry. Your imprudence will soon be forgotten," Lady Morton assured me. "Every season, a young debut disgraces herself." I wanted to correct Lady Morton that I was far from a debutante. "But a prudent match," she pressed on without allowing me to wedge in an objection, "and a sensible husband would soon remedy any shortcomings on your part."

Under Lady Morton's onslaught, I was beginning to fear that young eligible bachelors, and their mothers, were willing to overlook my educational transgressions, especially since a large sum of money had been settled on my name.

I returned my gaze to the more pleasant view outside. In between avoiding my mother's matrimonial plans, I was not opposed to having a bit of fun. Just this New Year's, I had taken part in a series of delightful scavenger hunts through London, made notorious by the press.

And truth be told, it was because of the outcome of one of these scavenger hunts that I was now making my way on The Blue Train, down to the French Riviera, in the decidedly unglamourous month of April.

For my parent's generation, the Riviera season began in January and ended promptly on May 1st, so that daughters could be presented at court at the spring ball. The Riviera was a place for convalescence or an opportunity to play tennis outdoors during the winter months.

But a couple of years ago, the Murphys, Gerald and Sara, from America, discovered the delights of the Cote d'Azur in the summer. They made the Riviera the place to be from late May to early September with beach parties, beach pajamas, cocktails, gramophones, and suntanning.

Alas, I was to have none of that, and not only because I was at least a month too early to the party.

My latest scavenger hunt adventure had culminated, to high society's horror, in a stint at a secretarial course in London. And while I didn't see why acquiring the skill of typewriting was such a bad indiscretion, my mother feared the social consequences of associating with shop-keepers' daughters deeply. The scandal of having a daughter of a peer learning to be a typist proved to be too much for her.

My mother, Lady Beasley, was a woman of formidable character and inexplicable contradictions. A daughter of a Boston Brahmin, a staunch federalist, whose ancestors hailed from the *Mayflower*, and had fought in the Battle of Princeton, she nevertheless embraced unreservedly the noble title bestowed upon her through her marriage to my father, and followed British aristocratic norms unfailingly.

Whenever I reproached her, she defended herself against my accusations of duplicity by saying she was, above all, a pragmatist and one would be a fool to cast aside the privileges of a title for such a trifle as a conscience.

Thus locked in an eternal battle, my mother and I had reached an impasse. The family convened to discuss what was to be done with me. The corruptive power of ready cash—so foolishly settled on me in the form of a sizable inheritance when I'd come of age four years ago

—was discussed at length, elucidated by Victorian sensibilities.

Simply allowing a young, and unmarried, woman to spend her money as she pleased was considered unseemly. Proper etiquette dictated that that was a husband's job.

But as I was proving to be a master of avoiding marriage, a socially acceptable solution was sought.

Rescue came from the unlikely quarters of my three aging paternal aunts, who, through no fault of their own, had arrived at the sage conclusion that a woman in possession of a good fortune would be ill advised to share it with a man.

The eminent family tree was shaken and out fell Uncle Albert, my father's second cousin, once removed, who was strong-armed into accepting his family duty. His fate for the foreseeable future was pre-determined by my three aunts, who, like the three witches of Macbeth, charted his destiny, namely, to dismiss his current secretary and hire me as his replacement.

The deal was sweetened by the fact that, as I had my own fortune, he didn't have to pay me. My uncle, who was otherwise completely batty in a typically English fashion, was able to recognize a good deal when he saw one, and engaged me without an objection.

It was in my new capacity as his secretary that I was now traveling to join him on the Riviera.

Sending me to my uncle was not an ideal outcome in my mother's eyes, but satisfactory on many levels—I was relegated to a dull corner of the globe, in the care of a male relative, long enough that my faux pas with the typing school could be forgotten and the scandal could blow over.

The arrangement suited me fine.

While visiting my maternal grandparents in Boston during the summers, and spending carefree months on their estate on Cape Cod, I had become acutely aware that women were quite capable of running big companies. Their neighbor, Marjorie Merriweather Post, for example, was at the helm of the Postum Cereal Company. And gossip magazines gushed over the latest millinery or dress shops established by mistresses of various rich men.

I couldn't understand why the only expectation for a woman like me—well educated and of good social standing—was marriage. I had my own money, and thus ready access to capital for a business, and I couldn't see why I had to bet my fortune on a husband who would squander it away on gambling or a mistress. Or most likely both.

And while my mother, as the daughter of an American industrialist, had the fortitude and determination to run her own company, the only thing she chose to run was my father's life.

A politician with no strong opinions, except the ones professed by my mother, my father had been henpecked into complete submission. My mother told him what to say, what to think, and who to invite to dinners and parties. In short, my mother controlled the politics of our shire from the mahogany table in our dining room.

I was perfectly determined to avoid marriage and kids.

Plus, my elder sister, Theodora, didn't seem to shy away from her ancestral duty of producing heirs. She had taken on the challenge with aplomb and was now on blighter number three.

A chill ran down my spine and not only because Lady Morton was surveying me unreservedly.

No, I mused, working for my uncle was not the punishment my mother had envisioned. It was a step in the right direction, if I wanted to one day run my own business.

But as Lady Morton droned on about Cecil—his job at the bank and his tennis game—and as we got closer to Nice, and as the scenery grew more exotic and the sky ever brighter, my thoughts darken. My mother's machinations and Lady Morton's ambitions were threatening to spoil an adventure I was quite looking forward to.

CHAPTER 2

The driver pulled up to Hotel Paradis. As grand as any in Europe, occupying a prominent position on Promenade des Anglais, and with a copper dome that dominated the landscape, it was the destination of choice in Nice.

The hotel's elegant white facade felt familiar and welcoming. I had memories of many happy moments with my family here. And while just a few years ago I would have been elated to be arriving at its doors, I now turned my eyes to the coast.

I gazed longingly towards the rocky cliffs, and the white villas, which, although I could not see, I imagined springing up on them quicker than fungi after rain. Young people were not staying in stuffy Belle Epoque hotels any longer, and I longed to be with my set in a white villa overlooking the sea.

"Welcome, Lady Caroline!" The hotel manager, M. Francois, swooped down the stairs in my direction. His manners were as impeccable as his suit. Undoubtedly, my mother had telephoned him personally to alert him of my arrival.

"Lady Morton," he turned politely to my companion from the train station, and with a snap of his fingers, in a trick worthy of a magician, his shadow split and out of it appeared his understudy —a young man, equally as sleek. The assistant manager was dispatched to assist Lady Morton.

With a second snap of his fingers, various uniformed men scrambled into a frenzy to offload luggage.

One had to give M. Francois credit; he ran his hotel with an acute understanding of the social peculiarities of the British peerage. He had made a calculated decision to cater personally to me, not solely based on my title. Hotels along the Riviera vied for my mother's business. While my mother was always overbearing and demanding during her stays, her lavish gratuities upon departure prevented the formation of any lasting resentment among the staff. And, more importantly, her stay drew the custom of other peers of the realm.

"And is your maid to follow?" M. Francois inquired. He cast a furtive look at the suitcases streaming past him.

"Oh no, M. Francois. I am to be my uncle's secretary and my own woman." I felt liberated saying that. After all, wasn't that why women had cut their hair into stylish bobs, so they wouldn't need a maid to brush their unpractically long hair for them?

He nodded his understanding. I smiled and

shrugged.

And as we ascended the stairs of the hotel, we entered into a conversation on matters of mother and country.

M. Francois helped me check in and was about to walk me to my suite when a man barred my way.

"Caroline?" the man said.

I looked up, startled. I didn't expect to see anyone here from my set.

"James!" I exclaimed.

The sight of James suddenly changed my attitude towards my stay on the Riviera. I was not condemned to evenings with Lady Morton and her Cecil, after all.

James was a friend of my late brother, Charles. They had been at Cambridge together, but I hadn't seen him since my brother's funeral. While always handsome, his face had changed in the last five, no, it had been seven years. His gentle features were now more angular and manly. His wavy sandy hair was swept to the side with a roguish confidence, and his clear blue eyes studied my face.

For a brief moment, I wondered what my brother would have looked like were he still alive. The title that had once been destined for Charles now went to my younger brother, Edward, who was currently at some club or other in London, drinking himself into a stupor, unwilling to accept the new reality and its accompanying responsibilities. I guess, in a way, neither was I.

"It's been ages," I gushed, shaking my dark thoughts away, and plastering on a smile. "What have you been doing with yourself?"

"Not much," he replied.

While I was delighted to see him, I could sense a definite chill in his manner. I wondered about its cause. Perhaps I reminded him of my brother and the war.

"Are you down for the winter?" I asked. "I would love to have a friendly face around."

"I am," he replied, still coldly.

I faltered, unsure how to proceed. I had not expected such a guarded reception from one of my brother's oldest friends, but decided to press on. "I'm here to be my Uncle Albert's secretary." *Isn't that such fun?* I wanted to add, but something in his manner stopped me.

"I know."

"Oh," was all I could reply, taken aback at how fast news traveled. "Tell me you're not one of those people who disapproves of a young woman working? You don't subscribe to the opinion that a woman working is stealing the bread of a deserving man?" I teased.

"Not at all. But as it happens, in this case, you have taken mine."

"What?" I replied. I didn't follow.

"I was your uncle's secretary until family obligations forced him to dismiss me." I didn't like how he put it.

For the first time since setting off on my journey, I felt a pang of regret. I had not dwelt on the fact that my uncle would have to dismiss his old secretary in order to engage me. And if the thought did cross my mind, I relegated the nameless and faceless secretary to that category of people one never thinks about, like people who deliver coal.

But here I was now, face to face with my uncle's former secretary. Not only did he have a face—a handsome one—and a name, but he was also an old friend. How was it I had not known that James was my uncle's secretary?

Then again, I never really thought about James that much. A few years older than me, our paths did not cross socially. He didn't strike me as a man who would go in for scavenger hunts and costume parties. I had always assumed that the reason we didn't run into each other socially was because he had his own set of friends, frequented his own London club, and was invited to different country house parties.

Plus, as the son of a peer himself, I never considered that he would need to work. But now it dawned on me that his absence from the social scene was perhaps due to being employed. I wondered how long he had worked for my uncle.

While all of these thoughts were swirling in my head, all I could say was, "I'm sorry. I didn't realize."

"Well, for some of us, work is not a game," he said, with more of a sigh than a reprimand.

"That is unkind," I chastised him, and quickly regretted it. He was not one of my chums whom I could freely criticize.

"You are quite right. I apologize," he said with a curt bow.

An idea formed in my head. "Listen, you are quite right. I should not have used my influence to secure this position. It is rightfully yours. I'm sure my uncle will be more than happy to have you back. We can just pop upstairs to his suite and explain the situation to him."

It pained me to give up a job before I had even started it, but it was the right thing to do. And perhaps, with some luck, my aunts could find another hapless uncle languishing on an old branch of the family tree; one who was not currently employing a secretary, but one who could be persuaded he needed one immediately.

"That would not be necessary. I've already secured a new post."

"So quickly!" I exclaimed, unthinking, then corrected myself, "I hope you find your new position satisfactory. By the way, what is my uncle like to work for?"

James smiled for the first time since our conversation started. "He's a pleasant gentleman, though a bit eccentric, in the manner expected for his age and position in life. But well within the boundaries."

I smiled and nodded. I understood. Growing up, Uncle Albert had rarely been around. His government posts took him to every corner of the empire. And I was sure he had picked up many quirks and customs along the way.

"Does he wear a velvet smoking jacket with toggle fastenings?" I asked.

"Invariably."

"And the requisite embroidered smoking cap topped with a tassel?"

"A fez, handmade in Cairo, but very much furnished with a tassel," James said, and spared me another smile.

"Well, it was nice to see you," I said. I was aware that M. Francois was still waiting for me in the wings. "I better go up to see my uncle and then settle in. Will you be staying at the hotel, or is your new employer spending the season elsewhere?" My mind jumped to the chic villas along the coast.

"Lord Packenham is also staying at the hotel. As are all the members of the Society, including your uncle. Except, of course, Count Karowsky. The members tend not to stray too far away from the prize."

Society? Prize? I had no idea what James was talking about. It seemed more urgent than ever to go up and acquaint myself with my duties.

"Well, cheerio!" I said.

"Actually," James said, looking slightly uncomfortable, "as your uncle's outgoing secretary, I am required to show you around and explain the responsibilities."

"Oh, of course!" How silly of me, I wanted to add. I regretted how badly our meeting was going.

Upon seeing James just now, a spark of hope had passed through me. He was a friendly face, someone my age with whom to lounge at the beach or spend evenings in Monaco. But the more James spoke, the more it became apparent that he wished to have nothing to do with me. His stiff manner, his short answers, his reference to "games", made it clear that he disapproved of me and my behavior.

Such conduct from anyone else would not have mattered, but it rankled coming from James. I have to admit that when I was younger, and my brother Charles would come home from university and bring James along, I used to make up silly excuses to be in James' company.

I wondered if, with time, he would forgive me for usurping his post, and we could go back to being chums.

CHAPTER 3

Before we could take the lift to my uncle's suite, however, a shrill cry pierced the refined air of the hotel lobby.

I turned in the direction of the scream.

The bustle of the atrium had stopped in its tracks. Bell boys, their brass-arched trolleys laden with trunks, suitcases, and travel cases, stacked several stories high, had halted. Others, with towers of boxes—containing new hats and shoes for tonight's outing to Monte Carlo's casino—balanced precariously in their arms, had paused to take a better look.

All stood gawking at the center of the atrium.

The only sound was the crystal chandelier, tinkling with the force of the cry. Much like in an earthquake, the delicate pendalogues measured out the force of the cry, amplified by the smooth marble walls and floor.

Under the multi-tiered chandelier, two women, dressed in an exuberance of furs, feathers and lace, stared at each other.

We onlookers stood there, silent, aware that we were witnessing two forces of nature colliding.

It was like watching the swelling of a summer storm. Having seen the first flash of lightning and heard the first rip of thunder, we waited for the gathered dark clouds to unleash the pent-up storm.

And then the break came. The two women unchained their fury and began arguing at the top of their voices in French.

The hotel manager, who had been hovering in the vicinity waiting for my conversation with James to conclude, excused himself and glided over to the spectacle.

I stared at the two women, aghast, certain that feathers were about to fly.

Although copious amounts of makeup hid and distorted each woman's features, I made an educated guess that the one wearing the thicker mask, and the more outrageous plumes, was older. While older, she struck me as the prettier one. With blond curls and pink cheeks, she made me think of a porcelain doll.

Her younger adversary, while equally embellished, had an air of viciousness which marred her pretty features.

M. Francois' intervention seemed not entirely successful, as the two women continued to glare at each other. Just then, a strapping young man, tall, dark and handsome, in an impeccable ivory day suit and artistically swept back hair, approached the younger of the two ladies, and, with a series of gallantries and bows, led her away from the conflict.

As they passed by me, I marveled at the man's expertise at dissipating the situation. He drew the woman's attention away from the squabble with polite questions about her plans for the day and pleasant compliments about her perfume.

I had to agree with him. Despite the woman's garish outfit, her perfume was fresh, crisp, and modern.

With the argument now over, having passed as quickly as a summer's thunderstorm, the buzz in the grand foyer resumed, and the manager approached me once again. I wanted to ask him about what we had just witnessed, but such nosiness was most unbecoming and unladylike.

And in any case, he spoke first. "If you permit me, a word before you go up to your suite. A package arrived from Switzerland and we have attended to it as instructed, but Chef Bernard is at a loss on how to serve the breakfast granules."

I smiled. I could just picture the hotel's chef puzzling over the nature of my Swiss breakfast muesli.

"And if you could give me similar instructions," the manager continued with deference, "as to the triangular candy bars, which were also in the box?"

"Oh, those! Those are the most wonderful

chocolate bars, M. Francois!" I gushed over the Toblerone bars I'd had shipped from Switzerland in addition to the breakfast muesli. "In fact, M. Francois, you should try one. Please, save a bar for yourself from my box and have the rest delivered to my suite with the luggage."

"You are too kind," he said and bowed. I doubted he appreciated my gesture at the moment, but I knew that when he tried the delicious milk chocolate, nougat and honey concoction, he would be converted.

James had witnessed the entire exchange, and I noticed his incredulous eyebrows rising ever higher on his face. But he was too much of a gentleman to say anything. And I was not about to give an unbidden explanation of my quirks and indulgences to a man, especially one who had slighted me.

With a shrug and a wide smile, I gave James to understand that the matter was not up for discussion. I knew my smile, with its straight white teeth and red painted lips, usually had a stimulating effect on men, and they seemed to follow suit whenever I brandished my grin.

But if the scowl on his face was anything to go by, I could not be sure my smile had the same effect on James. With a heavy sigh, I trudged in his wake to the lift and up to Uncle Albert's rooms.

And although James' attitude weighed heavily on my mind, it was thoughts of the two ladies arguing that kept popping up in it. What offense could have brought about such behavior, such humiliating spectacle, and such public display of anger? Mostly, I felt sorry for M. Francois, who always aspired to make the hotel the most respectable place in Nice.

CHAPTER 4

"Ah, young Carol and young James. What can I help you with, young birds?" Uncle Albert greeted us as we entered his suite.

Any thoughts of ladies with feathers in their hats disappeared as I blushed. Could the old man think James and I were a couple?

"Lady Caroline is here to take over responsibilities as your secretary. We discussed the change at length, if you recall?" James said.

"Oh, that's right, that's right," my uncle said, and waved me in, inviting me to step further into the room. "Come in, my child, and sit here," he indicated a chair by his side.

The room was luxuriously but tastefully furnished, with a Louis XIV desk, a fine example of a *bureau plat*, in the middle. My uncle, however, was not seated at the desk, but on a sofa of the same period, with his left foot up on a gilded pouf.

"Now, don't let young James fool you," my uncle continued. "Forget all this letter writing mumbo jumbo. The job at hand, at the moment, is the location of the—". My uncle stopped abruptly and turned to James. "Since you are now employed by my rival and bitter enemy, James, I think it's time for you to leave, so Caroline and I can plan our strategy."

I had no idea what Uncle Albert was talking about, so I sent a desperate look towards James, hoping to convey my confusion. But he just smiled and bowed on his way out, as Wilford, my uncle's man, closed the door behind him.

"Now, and this is most important," my uncle turned his attention to me, "how is your stamina? I hear you've been leading in the scavenger hunt races." I smiled demurely. He clapped. "Capital! The old gout is biting at the big toe at the moment," he looked critically at the foot on the pouf, "so I cannot traipse around the cliffs as I used to."

I gazed at my uncle. While his eyes were bright and alert, his stooped shoulders and general pudginess made me doubt that even on a good day he could get further than the hotel lobby.

"Now, young Carol, ignore everything young James has told you. He now works for the competition. Old Lord Packenham is a first class scoundrel and a cheat, and I have no doubt that he will get James to throw the match. But Lord Fetherly is the one to watch. He's got himself a secretary from Switzerland, and apparently as crooked as they come. The other members of our little Society are old fogies and are of no consequence. Only that young Frenchman—or is he Dutch?—might pose a threat, but he is too ambitious to compromise his standing in the Society by claiming the prize himself."

I needed to step back. I had no idea what Uncle Albert was talking about. It sounded more complex than the troop movements before the Somme battle.

He had just paused to take a breath, and I saw my opportunity. "Dear uncle, but I have no idea what you are talking about."

"Why, about the annual prize of the Royal Society for Natural History Appreciation, of course. The Golden Platypus!"

He looked around. "Wilford!" He turned as far as his old spine would allow him. "Wilford," he called again, and then spotted his man standing, waiting by his elbow. "Ah, there you are. Take young Carol here to see the prize. I would do it myself, but the old toe, you see." He pointed to the extended foot.

"Very good, My Lord."

We rode the lift down in silence, and I followed Wilford to a display case hidden in a corner of the lobby.

"The Golden Platypus, My Lady," he said, and stepped aside to reveal the prize enclosed in the display cabinet.

I had no idea how he had managed to keep a straight face delivering that last line. I turned to him with an enquiring eyebrow, but his face was a stony fortress. If there were any uncharitable thoughts behind its wall, he was not about to surrender them.

"Is this a joke?"

"I can assure you that this item lies at the very center of your uncle's heart's desire."

I leaned in to study the specimen more closely. If what Wilford was saying was true, then beauty truly did rest in the eye of the beholder. Or perhaps, in this case, the adage that love is blind might have been more apt at explaining away the follies of aged men.

"Wilford," I addressed him, assuming that, like any sane person, he comprehended the absurdity of what we were observing, "this is the most pathetic thing I have seen!"

He remained silent, and we both turned to gaze at the prize.

Sitting at the bottom of the display case was an ebony base, with an ornate brass plaque engraved with the animal's exalted honorific. Perched atop it was the most pitiful example of a stuffed animal. I stared at it for a few moments. My uncle had been sure that one look at this trophy would explain it all, but in fact, in light of the moth-eaten pile of fur contained in the display case, what my uncle had said made even less sense than before.

"If you permit me," Wilford said placidly after a few moments, "I may be able to throw some light on the matter."

"Please, do," I replied eagerly.

"It is my understanding that the value of this award lies in the intangible, rather than what the eye perceives. It is one of the oldest stuffed specimens of *Ornithorhynchus anatinus*, commonly known as the duck-billed platypus. The specimen's 'golden' epithet refers to the singular hue of its fur."

I turned to look at the animal again. Indeed, the pale fur, as though bleached by the sun, was one of its most pathetic features. The bald spots, and generally unkempt appearance, its others.

"As you no doubt know, this is not the natural color of this species. The specimen owes its unlikely tone to questionable 18th century preservation and taxidermy techniques. The fact that it also spent an entire year in Lord Abington's south-facing drawing room, did not help the matter. The glabrous spots, that have probably caught your attention, were caused by Lord Fetherly's spirited Airedale Terrier, Bunny, getting a hold of the creature when the prize was in his possession a few years back. And the singed ends along its face can be attributed to Lord Mantelbury's maid, Gladys, mistaking the trophy for a large rat and throwing it in the fire after clobbering it with an iron poker."

"And this is the prize for which the members of the Royal Society for Natural History Appreciation are competing?" I asked, trying to keep my voice level.

"It would appear so, My Lady." Wilford stepped back from the display case, as though to permit me a better view of the prize at its bottom.

"I've seen enough," I said to him.

He bowed slightly and led the way back to the lift.

"I have seen the prize," I addressed Wilford as we rode the lift up, "but I still do not understand how it concerns me."

"I believe the intricacies of the current competition would best be elucidated by your uncle, but if I may give you a brief introduction, every year the members of the Society—"

"And who are the members?"

"The membership is large, but attendance varies depending on the desirability of the appointed destination. Currently, in addition to your uncle, the attendees include Lords Abington, Fetherly, Mantelbury, and Packenham. And also the gentleman whom your uncle referred to alternatively as a Frenchman or a Dutchman. I believe he is neither, but is in fact a Polish Count, Count Karowsky.

"The prize has eluded your uncle for several years, and he is most desperate to bring home the gold, so to speak. And if I may be permitted to say so, I believe your scavenger hunt prowess will be an asset to your uncle."

"Thank you Wilford. That is very kind."

While Oxford University had been a diverting place to practice Ancient Greek and discuss the emergent philosophies of logical positivism and phenomenology, while still throwing in a good game of tennis, it was my spell at Frau Baumgartnerhoff's finishing school in Switzerland that has given me the skills I've found most useful in life up to now.

Recently divorced, Frau Baumgartnerhoff had thrown out the conventional syllabus centered around proper decorum, and instead had endeavored to instill in her girls a sense of self-reliance. To that end she educated us in the art of mountaineering, orienteering and hiking. No more were we to be helpless and hapless damsels stuck on a steep slope of a mountain, waiting to be rescued by a burly mountain man. Give us a pick and a bit of rope and we were going to overcome any obstacle that stood in our way. Or so the theory went.

Those skills proved indispensable to me in London—I could read the tube map or scale a courtyard wall faster than any other girl—and were the principal reason behind my scavenger hunt success. It now seemed as if those same skills, given Wilford's compliment, would serve me well on the Riviera.

Emboldened by the old valet's words, upon returning to my uncle's suite, I found myself perched on the edge of a chair near my uncle's right elbow, notebook in lap, pencil poised, eager to take down notes.

"Now, young Carol, the rules of the contest are simple. The first to spot a blooming *Neotinea lactea*, known to you no doubt as a milky orchid, this spring, will win The Golden Platypus."

I nodded and took down the name.

"What makes it so special?"

"It's a temperamental little blighter," my uncle said, chuckling, as though talking about an endearing stripling.

I wrinkled my nose. That did not sound like an encouraging description of a flower. "How will I recognize it?"

"It's a small-sized species, and can be identified by its trilobed labellum dotted with purple, and its greenish helmet veined with purple on the inside."

As my eyes glazed over, I decided to get to the heart of the matter. "And where does this orchid grow?"

"Now, that's the exciting bit. You need to keep in mind while searching for it, that it enjoys growing in siliceous as well as calcareous soil." He fumbled with some papers on a table by his left elbow and came up with a small diary. "The temperature, and hours of sunshine, I've been making a record in my book," he said, leafing through it, "have been just right. It will bloom any day now." He turned to me with an expression that told me we were about to discuss serious matters. "Now, the thing to do to ensure victory is to locate it."

I would have thought that was obvious, but instead said, "How does one do that?"

"Ah, that is the question. My research indicates that the flat-winged bumblebee makes its underground nest in burrows near the flowers. So the trick is to locate the bumblebee before the flower blooms. You will have to traverse the southernmost hills, facing due south, but with a prevailing westerly breeze, and poke around with a stick."

"Why?" I grimaced, distrusting the stick part.

"The stick will allow you to prod awake the flat-winged bumblebee from its winter slumber. They are just waking up and quite lethargic."

The more my uncle spoke about the mission, the more I sank down in my chair. I could just visualize myself plodding across the sea cliffs, prodding the ground for bumblebees. It sounded to me like a perfect plan to get stung or fall off a cliff, or both, as in fall off a cliff after getting stung.

But I was not one to shy away from family duty.

"And you are saying that all the other members of the Society will be out on the bluffs, prodding for bumblebees?" I asked.

My uncle laughed wholeheartedly. "No, of

course not. It's their secretaries who will."

CHAPTER 5

That settled it. If the other secretaries could do it, so could I. And let the best woman win.

I left Uncle Albert's rooms, giving a silent thanks to Frau Baumgartnerhoff for having prepared me for just such an occasion, and went to find out whether my maid had had the foresight to pack a sturdier pair of shoes.

By teatime, I was full of determination. First, I was determined to win that hideous prize and second, upon entering the terrace, I became determined to avoid Lady Morton, whose hat I could spot hovering over one of the tables.

I observed the guests gathered on the terrace this afternoon, and came to the realization that the hotel was devoid of young people. Instead, it was full of matrons on the Riviera for convalescence.

Judging by the looks they sent my way, these were matrons looking to marry off their sons. As I walked between the tables and exchanged polite nods, I could practically feel their eyes sizing me up and calculating whether a match was in the stars.

No doubt Lady Morton had informed the rest of her peers of the degradation of my matrimonial stock. If she had been a more guarded woman, she would have kept that ace closer to her ample bosom. But no doubt Lady Morton was so assured of her success, and Cecil's, that she couldn't resist crowing about it to her friends.

I let the gentle breeze of the Mediterranean and the honeyed notes of mimosa wash over me and drive away unpleasant thoughts.

"Beastly!" The unexpected war cry hit me in the back of the neck like a wayward golf ball.

I instantly knew who it was and turned around to witness the hefty shape of Persephone "Poppy" Kettering-Thrapston, parting the crowds.

Poppy—I'm ashamed to admit that I did not have a witty sobriquet equivalent to her corruption of my family name, but perhaps, given the original, in her case one was not required—had been Head Girl at Boughton Monchelsea School for Girls, near Boughton under Blean, if you know it, housed in the 13th century ancestral home of William de Monti, and last renovated at around the same time, where I had gone to school.

She was a loud, capable girl who went in for all the sports. Her double barrel name came from the union of two adjacent landed families, who had joined forces to oppress the local populace of a small region just south of the cathedral city of Peterborough with consolidated gusto.

Poppy retained all the chief character traits of her family—she was a bully and used to getting her own way. I always wondered if, when she got married, they would add another hyphen to the current mouthful.

And while she insisted on calling everyone by their nickname, I was willing to overlook that fact now. Although not at the top of my Christmas list, Poppy was a chum from school, and we ran in the same social circle. I was glad to see someone my own age at the hotel.

"Now, Gassy," she said, as she barreled towards me and tucked me under her elbow, "I heard about your London escapade and your banishment to the Riviera. But fear not, I have drawn up a program of activities."

And if you are wondering about my nickname, Gassy, it's a corruption of my other nickname, Beastly, which in itself is a corruption of my family name, Beasley. It's Beasley, as in beastly, as in ghastly, as in gassy. You get the point. Poppy saved 'Gassy' only for when she was feeling particularly chummy.

"I wish you wouldn't call me Gassy. We are adult women," I said demurely. In Poppy's presence, I was back at school, wearing knee socks.

But Poppy just dismissed me with a laugh. I knew that to Poppy, nicknames were part of the social structure. It was what separated our set from the bourgeoisie and the proletariat.

Many a sleepless night at school, in our dorm room with my chums, was spent trying to come up with suitable sobriquets for Poppy—Plonker, Plague, Ploppy—but since none of us dared call her those to her face, they never caught on.

In true Poppy fashion, she had secured the best table on the terrace. Situated under a voluminous mimosa, which cast ample shade, it had an uninterrupted view of the blue Mediterranean beyond.

"Gassy, I was glad when I heard you were coming down to spend time with your uncle. Have a seat," she said in her clipped sergeant-major manner, which always signaled a plan. "It's good for me to have company while I'm here, and I have a few fun things planned for us this week."

She paused to stack her plate with pastries.

"I gave you the night off tonight to settle in," she pressed on, "but tomorrow is a beach day, followed by dinner at Chez Vincent, and Monte Carlo. I've arranged a car to take us down to Juan-Les-Pins in the morning."

I perked up. Juan-Les-Pins was the place to be, even if it was a bit out of season. I needed to find a way to both go to Juan-Les-Pins and do my uncle's bidding. Which put me to mind of something I had meant to ask Poppy.

"Poppy, how come you are here so early in the

season? I mean, most of our lot now comes after May." Poppy had always been one to follow trends, and I didn't expect her to have missed the shift in fashionable time to be seen on the Riviera for the under 30s.

"Oh, that," she waved my question off, "daddy has sent me down ahead of him with Nanny." She pointed to the old woman in a plain black frock dozing in a lounge chair under an umbrella further down on the verandah. Poppy's mother had died while Poppy was still young, so her Nanny and her father had brought her up. Perhaps it explained some of her character. "I'm to meet with M. Arnold. You know, the of-the-moment villa architect. I am to spend the week driving up and down the coast with him to pick the ideal location for a villa."

"What?" I gaped. That was a serious undertaking.

"Yes," she nodded, with a bit of glee in her eye due to the shock she had caused. "Daddy thinks that a villa on the Riviera will make me more eligible."

I furrowed my brow. Not short on funds herself, Poppy had admitted more than once that she was on the lookout to snag a beau who would improve the family stock in the looks department. No Cecils for her.

Despite all her shortcomings, I liked Poppy's no nonsense attitude towards life.

But her desire to marry someone tall, dark and handsome, like a young Rudolf Valentino, with Adonis proportions, was impeded by her failure to resemble her namesake Persephone. Matters were complicated by the fact that her father was a shrewd businessman and he would not allow a match with some money-grabbing cad. Someone like Cecil was more Poppy's speed, but she would not even spare him a glance. So she remained unattached.

"Gone are the ghastly Belle Epoque villas and all their superfluous frills. So last century. The war has taught us all about the value of simplicity. It's all about straight lines, and sharp angles," said Poppy. "M. Arnold is the one to go with on the Riviera if you desire the latest design. Plus, he's a bit of a dish—"

At that moment, Poppy became distracted. She threw a demure smile in the direction of a table to the left.

CHAPTER 6

I followed Poppy's gaze and saw two handsome and elegant young men. One was the man from this morning, who had managed to separate the two ladies so gallantly.

I leaned in towards Poppy. "Who are those men?"

"The one with the perfect hair and the canary yellow cravat," I could see she was referring to the man from this morning, "is Count Karowsky. A florist—grows exotic flowers in greenhouses. He works with M. Arnold on most of the villa projects. Sitting with him,"—I looked discreetly at the other man. Although less debonair, he was sporting a well-tailored suit and a well-tended mustache—"is Baron Tacotti, an infamous, or at least greatly suspected, jewel thief."

I gasped. "You shouldn't believe all the rumors," I said.

"Well then, how do you explain the string of robberies at villas on the Riviera?" she asked, but didn't wait for my reply. "Isn't he dreamy?" she said and gazed in the gentlemen's direction.

"Poppy," I chastised her, but giggled, "you know your father would never allow it."

"No, but a girl could dream."

She twinkled her fingers in the direction of the Baron and the Count. I wondered if the rings on her fingers, catching the afternoon rays with such vigor, were catching Baron Tacotti's attention. If he were a jewel thief, that is.

"At least you don't have to worry about that," Poppy turned to me.

"About what?"

"Well, you could marry anyone you want. Your looks would overcome any deficiencies in your husband's appearance."

"Even Cecil's?" I asked with a cocked eyebrow.

"Oh, yes," Poppy said in a subdued tone and looked in Lady Morton's direction. "It does seem that Lady Morton looks on the whole thing as *fait accompli*. What's your plan to wiggle out of this one?"

"Well, it's too much to hope that my father would put his foot down, and my education has not scared her away, so I only hope that by sticking by my uncle's side, I shall leave the Riviera for the Royal Society's next location before Cecil makes his way here. From what I've heard, my uncle and his cabal never stick around a place for more than a month, before decamping to the next exotic locale.

"On the whole, though, I don't think my mother would consider a union with Lady Morton's family advantageous, regardless of how close Lady Morton believes to me to my mother. But I think my mother would not discourage a Cecil onslaught, just to goad me."

But I was tired of talking and thinking about my mother, and looked for a change of topic. My eyes fell on Count Karowsky.

"So that's Count Karowsky? My uncle's man mentioned that the Count is part of my uncle's Society. I wonder what a young, handsome man is doing in the company of old fogies?"

"They might be fogies to you, but don't forget that every one of those old, dithering men is, or at least was, a titan of industry or government. Their connections and influence run deep in the fertile soil of the aristocracy. By all indications, Count Karowsky is not a fool."

"What exactly is his business?"

"He's of a bit of an uncertain pedigree, I hear, but now has the most fabulous greenhouses just outside of Grasse. Started just a couple of years ago, and now the whole hillside is covered in glass. Acclimatizes and breeds the most exotic of plants. He's the darling of all the new villa owners and has developed a close working relationship with M. Arnold. Everyone who gets a villa by Arnold, wants a garden by Karowsky." A faraway, misty look replaced her sane one, and she gazed in the direction of the table where the Count sat. "I hope we get many intimate moments together when we are planning my garden."

I pushed a piece of eclair around the plate. Poppy's directness made me blush a bit.

"But even if I find the perfect location for a villa, I would have to wait my turn. Currently he's busy planning a villa for Mlle Violette—"

"Who?"

"You know, one of the women in the foyer this morning."

"Were you there?"

"No, but word gets around."

"Which one? There were two causing the disturbance."

"The younger one. The other is Mlle Rosalie. She looks more like a Madam by now than a Mademoiselle, but that's neither here nor there. The important point is they are great rivals. Both had been star dancers at the 'Folies Bergere' in Paris. Mlle Rosalie is Lord Withermorlington's former mistress, Mlle Violette is his current one. Apparently, Lord Withermorlington has a soft spot for dancers from the Folies."

"That at least explains the theatrical costumes of both women."

Poppy nodded in agreement. "So, when Mlle Rosalie first became Lord Withermorlington's lover, Mlle Violette was still coming up the ranks of the dance troupe." She was spitting this information out in rapid succession. Poppy might have many faults, but her access to gossip was faultless.

"The clencher is," she pressed on at the same speed, "that Mlle Violette won Lord Withermorlington's favor before Mlle Rosalie's villa was completed. He stopped funding its completion because now he was bankrolling a new villa for Mlle Violette."

She paused for a breath, took a bite of her gateau, and plunged in again. "Word is, Mlle Violette is not only milking him for the villa, but is touching him to fund a business for her as well."

This made me perk up. "What kind of business?"

"Oh, I don't know. You know how these mistresses are. A dress boutique or a millinery, I guess."

I nodded. I knew exactly how it was.

"So you can see why Mlle Rosalie would have been so incensed at meeting Mlle Violette this morning," Poppy continued. "Not only was Mlle Violette able to get land and a villa out of him, but also a business. And Mlle Rosalie could not even get a completed villa. No wonder they hate each other so much."

"You mean Mlle Rosalie has nowhere to live?"

"No, I think the building itself is complete, but she doesn't have sufficient funds to furnish and landscape it to her lavish standard. Or at least she prefers not to use her own money when she can get a new suitor to foot the remaining bill. Although at her advanced age of 32, Mlle Rosalie is finding it more and more difficult to get suitors. These circumstances have forced her to appeal to old lovers, and she has been traveling to Italy, Switzerland and Germany to find a new patron. She had just returned this morning from her trip when she ran into Mlle Violette."

I could see what Poppy meant. It appeared that in the business of a mistress, taking heed of the saying 'make hay while the sun shines' was vital.

I hoped, for Mlle Violette's sake, that she would see her villa completed before Lord Withermorlington's next visit to the Folies in Paris.

CHAPTER 7

The next morning, the breakfast room was positively buzzing when I went in. I had spotted Lady Morton's location, and pretended not to see her trying to catch my eye as I made my way to Poppy's table. Uncle Albert, still incapacitated by his bout of gout, was breakfasting in his rooms.

As the waiter brought my muesli to the table, Poppy rushed to fill me in on overnight developments at the hotel.

Before she had a chance, M. Francois swooped down on our table with his signature curvet, a jump to rival any at the Paris Opera.

"Lady Caroline, Miss Kettering-Thrapston," he addressed each of us, accompanied by a curt bow. "Lady Caroline," he turned to me, "I am only too glad that nothing you had put away in the safe was stolen last night. I would not be able to face your mother if one of your jewels was ever stolen." He turned to Poppy. "And I am most grateful to whoever broke into the safe that none of your valuables were taken, Miss Kettering-Thrapston."

Is that why I had seen, on my way to breakfast, James sitting in the manager's office with two uniformed policemen? He'd closed the door upon seeing me. I now wondered if anything of Lord Packenham's had been stolen.

"What's happened, M. Francois?" I asked, still in the dark, but starting to get an inkling.

"Thank you for taking an interest in our troubles, Lady Caroline," he said, with a touch of drama, and dabbed his forehead with a monogrammed handkerchief to complete the sketch. "The safe in my office was broken into last night. I just don't understand it. Nothing appears to have been taken."

I scanned the room for Baron Tacotti. He was sitting by himself at a table to the side, the picture of all innocence. His hand did not shake as he lifted the small cup of coffee to his lips, then dabbed delicately at his sculpted mustache with the corner of his napkin. His dark eyes did not shy away from the looks thrown furtively in his direction by the breakfast guests, and he even seemed to return their gaze with humor in his eyes. Or at least it seemed so when he reached my gaze and caught me looking at him. He smiled politely and bowed his head. I returned his smile and looked away.

If the rumors about Baron Tacotti were true, he didn't seem troubled by them. Why would he break into the hotel safe, but not take any jewelry?

Perhaps the jewelry he was after was not in the safe, and he was not tempted by anything else?

As M. Francois walked away to conciliate another guest, Poppy leaned forward. "He's lying," she said.

"Who is?"

"The manager."

"M. Francois? What do you mean?"

"Well, rumor has it that some valuable papers appear to have been stolen. Papers belonging to Mlle Violette."

I cocked an eyebrow at Poppy and I looked slyly in the direction in which Poppy was openly glaring. Mlle Violette's demeanor was markedly different from yesterday, and from all the other guests at breakfast. While everyone else was busy gossiping, Mlle Violette was staring ashen-faced at her untouched breakfast, her eyes full of murder.

"How do you know?" I turned to Poppy.

"Mrs. Lockeridge told Mrs. Hamilton, who told Lady Nettleship, who, in turn, told Lady Morton, and you know Lady Morton has trouble keeping information to herself. And so it transpired that Mrs. Lockeridge has a suite on the same floor as Mlle Violette, fortuitously adjacent. Inadvertently, of course, she overheard—by pressing a glass on the wall, I am told—a conversation between the manager and Mlle Violette. I say conversation, but it appears Mlle Violette reprised her theatrics from yesterday morning."

Poppy paused and cast an appraising look at me to see if I had followed her meaning. Satisfied, she continued, "Mlle Violette was exceptionally distraught when the manager briefed her of the break-in, and even more so when he informed her that the letter she had deposited in his safe-keeping had gone missing."

I looked back at Mlle Violette and then to Baron Tacotti. It didn't appear that either was concerned with the other. Could Baron Tacotti be a blackmailer as well as a jewel thief?

"Do we know the nature of the letter?"

"Oh, something incriminating, I'm sure. Something a man would prefer his wife not to see. But no, I don't know any particulars."

"Was anything of Lord Packenham's taken?" I asked, thinking back to seeing James with the police.

"Not as far as I know. Why do you ask?" she said, narrowing her eyes at me.

"No, nothing," I quickly said. "I just wondered if any of the other hotel guests had something stolen." It was a poor coverup, but that was the best I could do. I preferred not to tell her about James. But I wondered all the same: If Lord Packenham was unaffected by the break-in, then what was James doing in the company of the police?

Poppy scrutinized me closely, but didn't press the subject. Instead, she returned her attention to our plan for the day.

While she was speaking, I wondered at how curious it was to break into a hotel safe and only take some letters. A revered establishment like the Hotel Paradis would hold in its steel bowels, at any given time, enough wealth to make even Louis XIV blush. What letters could be more valuable than jewels?

CHAPTER 8

A middle child, and a girl, my mother took no great notice of me until I was of marriageable age. My sister had married as expected, and my mother did not suppose I would be much trouble either. But then the great war happened, and it changed everything. The old social norms and expectations, all of a sudden, did not mean anything.

Men who had been groomed all their lives for great things, like my brother Charles, perished. I couldn't see the point of it all. Perhaps that was why I went in for scavenger hunts and parties. Perhaps at twenty-five, I was too old for games. But I just wanted to get away from it all.

I had been spared the worst of my mother's influence. Early on, while my brother Charles was still a baby, an English nanny, trained by the venerable Norlan College, had tried to establish authority over my mother in the nursery. No one has authority over my mother. The nanny was quickly dispensed with and an American one instilled in her place. So the tradition became that we were raised by American nannies. Not only did that affect our use of the English language, and we were all known to drop Americanisms from time to time, to the dismay of our British peers, but all of us Beasley children grew up with that great American character streak—individualism.

It was this streak of individualism that I was trying to employ in dealing with the competing priorities of the day. The thing required delicate balancing and divine inspiration.

There was Poppy's invitation—or was it more a command?—for a beach day. And I was determined to keep that appointment. But there was also Uncle Albert's correspondence and the hunt for the elusive bloom to be taken care of.

And I was not about to skive off on the first day of my new job, or on family responsibilities. Blood being thicker and all, after breakfast, I went up to my suite and found my suit—one of seven I'd had made especially for the occasion—already pressed by the maid, and trudged to my uncle's rooms looking the part of a secretary.

Although my uncle had impressed on me the importance of finding the orchid bloom over any other business, upon further questioning, it transpired that the bloom had to be searched for during full-sun hours, ideally at noon, with the sun beating down straight on one's head. I had hoped that I could search for the flower in the cool hours of the morning, but my uncle assured me I was looking for a sun-loving flower that opened its buds only in full sun. So in addition to the hazards of being stung by a bee and falling off a cliff, I now could pencil in heat-stroke as well.

So before I could figure out how to combine the responsibilities of beach-going with flower-hunting, I decided to tackle my uncle's correspondence.

Arriving at his suite, I found him in much the same position as the previous day. Upon enquiring after his toe, I got much the same answer. Apparently, the toe was still giving my uncle unwelcomed reminders of its presence.

As I made my way to his bureau, one look told me that my family had intervened just in time. I couldn't believe James had been so lax in attending to his duties. It was a good thing, it seemed, after all, that I was to be Uncle Albert's secretary. We had managed to nip the James problem in the bud.

"Uncle," I said, drawing his attention away from a botanical volume in his lap, "was James a satisfactory secretary?" I pointed an accusatory finger at three small mounds of unopened letters to underline my point.

"Adequate enough," he said.

"Was he particularly indifferent to answering your correspondence?"

"No, not particularly. I would actually say that he was quite capable."

Turning back to the unopened letters, I

wondered what the standards were among secretaries, if Uncle Albert considered James' rate of reply satisfactory. But perhaps James had left all these letters unanswered as an act of retaliation for being pushed out of his position.

"But uncle," I lamented, "he has left a week's worth of mail unanswered."

"What?" My uncle looked up again, and this time followed my unrelenting finger towards the piles of letters. "Ah, that," he said, with a calmness I was not feeling at the moment, "that's just yesterday's post, morning and evening, and this morning's. Wilford has just deposited them there for your perusal."

I sighed.

As succinct as my uncle was in his speech, so he was flowery in his responses to his correspondents. He insisted on discovering, no, *on employing*, the most appropriate adjectives for each occasion. But I would not be my mother's daughter if I could not excel at answering correspondence. So the letters were dispensed with and I was ready to tackle the beach.

I changed into a pair of chic French beach pajamas that had been made so popular recently by Mme Coco. The loose layers of silk felt divine against my skin, and I decided to forgo the use of the lift in favor of the grand staircase. As I glided down the stairs, feeling something of a wood nymph, I proceeded directly to M. Francois' office, sidestepping a few policemen, to take care of the minor matter of the flower hunt.

As M. Francois had been so kind to offer his and his staff's help in every matter, I explained my small problem to him. Post-haste, the noblest and brightest messenger boy, one with an intimate knowledge of the hills, hailing from a long line of goat herders, was summoned.

The boy looked intelligent and nodded eagerly in all the right places during my description of his responsibilities for the day. In retrospect, the eagerness might have arisen from the offer of five pounds, rather than an innate interest in botany.

But at the time, I considered his pedigree of communing with nature and prodding things with sticks, vis-a-vis the goats, as a boon for the task at hand. Uncle's prize was in the bag. And I wondered why no one else had thought of this scheme before.

I had a good feeling that I had left the hunt for the elusive bloom in the most capable of hands, and proceeded with a clear conscience toward Poppy and the waiting car. After all, local boys were better suited for traipsing over rugged cliffs while prodding things with sticks.

CHAPTER 9

Oh, the drive down to Juan-les-Pins was divine. The breeze on one's face, the warm sun, my substantial straw hat flapping in the wind.

Chef Bernard had prepared a sumptuous feast in a picnic basket, which we soon discovered to contain sandwiches, cold roast chicken, potato salad, fruits, a selection of pastries and slices of cake, bottles of lemonade, a bottle each of white, rose, and red wine, and a couple of bottles of the best champagne, even ice cream in a vacuum container. The driver had brought the basket down to the sand, together with a couple of beach lounges, a sun tent, and two umbrellas.

The season was still too early to meet any of the avant garde guests of the Murphys on the beach. But the region had become a favorite destination almost overnight, so much so that American millionaire Frank Jay Gould was building a hotel just down the coast, and a group of Americans—no doubt here to stake a claim on the best villa spots—was already here. And they had brought a gramophone with them, so the beach party was complete.

Towards the afternoon we had formed a large and rowdy circle, us sharing the bounty of our picnic basket and the Americans sharing their jazz music from the gramophone. The Toblerone bars I had brought were a hit, and many happy moments were spent watching people trying to eat around the uncomfortable triangular shape of the chocolate pieces. Poppy was in top form, flirting with every male specimen on the beach. It was jolly good fun.

I only spared the briefest of thoughts for James and wondered if he would be at the casino in the evening.

It was full of bonhomie and thoughts of more pleasure to be had at the casino later on in the evening, that we drove back to the hotel in the afternoon.

I had forgotten about my flower assignment until we pulled up under the hotel portico. And what I saw made my blood boil. There he was, the messenger boy from this morning, exchanging payment with Lord Mantelbury's secretary, no doubt selling him valuable information about his flower search and doubling his proceeds for the day.

"Come here, you scoundrel!" I steamrolled towards him. When he caught sight of me, he grabbed the bill from the secretary's hand, and ran for cover, and so did Lord Mantelbury's secretary.

Slinking away like a naked worm, instead of remaining at the scene of the crime, like a true gentleman, I immediately formed the most unfavorable impression of him.

But my beef was with the messenger boy. I hadn't climbed Alpine hills for nothing. I caught up with him in a few bounds, fortuitously aided by wearing pants and sport shoes. Under the stern eye inherited from my mother, the imp confessed that Lord Mantelbury's secretary had bribed him for information about the orchid. Luckily, however, the little blighter had discovered nothing, and had most likely spent the day lounging under the shade of a tree, anyway.

I had half a mind to walk him into M. Francois' office, but on second thought decided that this transgression would probably cost him his job, and causing a young boy's unemployment over a hideous stuffed water rat, especially when his family probably depended on the money, wasn't my thing. We had a stable boy back home who was supporting a sick mother and two young sisters. His father had died in the war.

So I gave the scoundrel in front of me a good talking to, which he didn't seem to notice, and dismissed him. Without payment, of course. He would have to console himself with his ill-gotten gains from Lord Mantelbury. But I didn't mention the incident to M. Francois.

As I walked back to my rooms, dark thoughts

clouded my brow. So it wasn't just Lord Fetherly, whom my uncle had warned me about, that one had to watch. It seemed Lord Mantelbury wasn't one to shy away from underhanded tactics either.

I considered my options. While I had no sympathy for the grotesque fur-bird in the display case, it obviously meant a lot to my uncle. And being incapacitated by his gout, he was completely relying on me to bring in the prize, so to speak.

By the time I had made my way to my suite, I had formulated a plan. I was not a champion sportswoman of the London scene for nothing. It seemed to me this search for an obscure orchid across the Riviera bluffs had all the hallmarks of a good game: convoluted clues, a dubious prize, and unworthy opponents.

In essence, this was a scavenger hunt. And I was very good at those.

The unfortunate incident with the messenger boy was forgotten. On reflection, it had been my fault. I had tried to pawn off of a task that was my responsibility on someone else. And as any true business manager knows, you should never delegate important work to people you don't know. I chalked it off to inexperience and shrugged it off.

I had a solid plan for tomorrow, with its own element of underhandedness. For its success, however, I would need my uncle's assistance. But that was all in the distant tomorrow. Tonight, I had a dinner with Poppy, and a night at the casino, to get ready for.

CHAPTER 10

By the time we assembled at the casino in Monte Carlo, it was clear that the younger people of the hotel were forming a jolly gang. Baron Tacotti and Count Karowsky were here, and so was Mlle Violette, who, I was glad to see, had recovered her pep from earlier. Perhaps the letter misadventure had resolved itself.

Next to her was a man Poppy introduced as M. Arnold. I had to agree with Poppy, his brand of charm was irresistible. While the Baron and the Count were both handsome, in a clean and wholesome way, helped along with copious hair pomade and scent, M. Arnold's handsomeness was enlivened by a certain devil-may-care twinkle in his eyes. He certainly looked fun to be around. And judging by the gaggle of young women in his vicinity, I wasn't the only woman to see it.

Walking around the casino rooms, I caught sight of a few of the Society's secretaries. I looked expectantly around for James before remembering that even if he was here, he would probably wish to avoid me.

Not a big gambler myself, I spent my time at the casino surveying its Belle Epoque lavishness. No amount of money had been spared to make people enjoy parting with theirs. The roulette room, with its grand glass cupola, crystal chandeliers, and gilded walls, was the busiest. Here the sound of the spinning roulettes and chasing balls was complemented by loud chatter and laughs. The gold and marble on the walls was matched by the feathers, beads, jewels, and fans of the patrons. Cocktails flowed, and no doubt contributed to the lively atmosphere. Swept up in the festivities, I ordered a glass of Martini myself.

Unexpectedly, the casino had another claim to fame. Four years ago, in 1921, the first women's olympiad was held in its gardens. I now made my way through the game salons, in search of the gardens, and found myself in the Salle Blanche, with its sweeping terrace overlooking the sea.

I saw James leave the salon for the gardens, and emboldened by my Martini, I followed him. His unreserved apathy towards me hurt. I still saw him as a friend. And I had longed to hear his memories of my brother, of things I didn't know, of their time together at university, even the war.

James was standing at the balustrade of the garden, overlooking the lower gardens and fountain. The air was warm and scented with the smell of white and purple flowers that give off their perfume at night. The noise from the casino was spilling out from the opened French doors, but the garden was peaceful and serene.

"James," I called out as I approached him.

He turned around abruptly, as though startled. "Caroline," he said curtly.

I wondered if he was expecting someone else. I walked up to the balustrade and leaned on it next to him. "Listen," I pressed on, undeterred by his bad manners, "I just wanted to apologize for taking your job."

"Yes, so you said." He cut my apology short. "No matter, I've got another."

We stood there in the night, each gazing ahead, at the fountain below and the sea beyond. I had never felt so awkward around James before. Perhaps seven years was a long time after all. But then again, it's not like James had made any effort to keep in touch with my family after my brother's funeral.

Unsure of how to proceed in the face of his indifference towards me, I decided to lighten the conversation. "Does the Royal Society always have such harebrained competitions?" I asked, laughing.

"Yes, almost exclusively," he said, but with no humor in his voice.

"Coming down on the train, I had these grand visions of being a proper secretary and corresponding with distinguished people on important matters. I never imagined that I would have to run around hills chasing a flower."

"I'm sorry the position doesn't live up to your expectations," James said, and I could see out of the corner of my eye that he had turned to look at my profile, searching.

No, that was not the way I had envisioned this conversation.

I turned to look at him as well. "That's not what I meant," I stammered, looking for a way to dig myself out of the hole. "I just meant that…" What had I meant? I wasn't even sure. I had just come out to talk to someone I thought was a friend, but it had all gone wrong. I reprimanded myself for even trying. If he were a true gentleman, he should have tried to approach me to make amends.

I could feel tears welling up in my eyes, and I turned away quickly. And suddenly, standing next to James, I thought of my brother, and I was sure I could not stop myself from crying. Blast it.

"Beastly, you are missing the most frightful fun!" Poppy yelled into the night.

I was happy for Poppy's opportune call. It saved me from making up a feeble excuse. James had made it abundantly clear that he didn't enjoy my company, and I saw no reason to stay where I wasn't wanted.

I turned to go, hurt, but tripped on a stone tile on the pathway. Cursing under my breath that I couldn't even make a dignified exit in James' company, I suddenly felt his hand take my arm to steady me on my feet. The gentle touch of his hand was in such stark contrast to his distant manner just moments ago.

For what felt like just a few breaths, he guided me down the path as though to make sure I was able to walk. But in those few moments I felt his other hand on the small of my back, his thumb touching the skin exposed by my low cut dress.

The contact sent electricity shooting up my spine and heat rose up my cheeks. Confused, I turned to him, but he withdrew his hand as though burned. I wondered if he had felt the electricity as well.

CHAPTER 11

The bustle of the casino swallowed me, and I was thankful for all the chatter, laughs and cries, which drove away my thoughts of James.

I made my way to Poppy, who was in the company of M. Arnold and Baron Tacotti.

I fell into conversation with the Baron, and it turned out that he—who, it transpired, was about my age, despite the old-fashioned mustache, but perhaps that was an Italian thing—had attended a boarding school in Switzerland. And as luck would have it, not far from my finishing school. Frau Baumgartnerhoff's establishment had been just above the village of St. Moritz, while Baron Tacotti's school, Laubanhamer School for Boys, was just a few miles away in Davos. We bonded over snow, hikes in the mountains, fresh milk and cheese from shepherds' huts, and Swiss chocolate.

Just as the Baron was telling me the most diverting story about a mountain goat on the school's roof during a particularly bad snowstorm, I caught sight of Mlle Rosalie. She was making her way across the room towards Mlle Violette on unsteady feet. Count Karowsky approached her, and attempted to prevent a renewed scene between the two women, but Mlle Rosalie, agitated, protested that she just wanted to talk, that she would not make a scene.

Pausing at a side table, Mlle Rosalie opened her bag, and for a moment, I admit it's silly, I thought she was about to take out a small revolver and shoot Mlle Violette. Instead, she retrieved a small packet, put whatever was in it in her drink, and consumed it in one gulp. Whatever was in the packet seemed to give her courage, because she then advanced closer to Mlle Violette.

A tense hush descended over our group. As the two ladies exchanged a few curt words, and sensing a new argument brewing, various men swooped in to separate them. Drinks were handed around to wash away animosities, and Count Karowsky, much like he had done with Mlle Violette the previous day, now led Mlle Rosalie to another room.

Baron Tacotti turned his attention to Mlle Violette.

By now, it was clear that everyone was a bit tipsy and M. Arnold seemed less guarded in his comments and in his assessment of the stakes at the card tables. M. Arnold's lady companions shrieked with growing regularity, signaling each time he lost another hand. By the sounds of it, he was on his way to losing all his profits from the night.

The losing streak must have directed his thoughts to money, or perhaps it was the diamond brooch he was now fingering, given to him by one of his lady companions to cover his latest loss, because he turned the conversation to the break-in at the hotel.

"What I cannot comprehend is how a hotel nowadays can have such an old-fashioned safe," he declared to our group. "It's an insult to the guests. Why would anyone deposit their valuables in it when any common thief can break in?" M. Arnold threw a meaningful look toward Baron Tacotti.

If the latter had heard the comment, he didn't show it. Something in Baron Tacotti's countenance made me conclude that he was probably very good at cards. But it was Mlle Violette that I pitied. M. Arnold's comment was most insensitive, especially given that Mlle Violette was standing within earshot of him.

Whether it was M. Arnold's thoughtless comment or meeting Mlle Rosalie again, it soon became apparent that Mlle Violette was not feeling well. She swayed in one spot and had to reach out to a side table to steady herself. She looked around, as though confused, her eyes glazed and unfocused. I feared that she'd had a bit too much to drink and might be sick at any moment.

I tried to catch Poppy's eye, but she was in conversation with M. Arnold, who had now abandoned the tables, and Count Karowsky, who must have abandoned his charge in the capable hands of another admirer and was back among our group. I looked around the room for Mlle Rosalie, but couldn't see her.

I leaned towards the group while keeping an eye on Mlle Violette. "Should we not limit Mlle Violette's drinks?"

"Oh, I wouldn't worry about it," M. Arnold said. "She always has a bit too much when Lord Withermorlington is not around. Lets loose, poor girl. She always has to be on best behavior around him." He winked at me.

But I was not convinced by his argument. Since I had an early morning ahead, I decided to call it a night and take Mlle Violette with me. There was no getting Poppy away from the men. As the night had stretched, her villa had grown bigger, and the garden ever more elaborate. No doubt, music to her companions' ears.

I searched with my eyes for Baron Tacotti, but couldn't see him. He must have had enough of M. Arnold and stepped away, I concluded.

As I made my way to a waiting car, a couple of casino workers supporting Mlle Violette, James appeared out of nowhere.

"I shall accompany you back to the hotel," he said without preamble.

I nodded, thankful to have another person with me. I'd dealt with drunk chums before, but it was nice to have an extra pair of hands in case we had to carry Mlle Violette.

We rode back to the hotel in silence. I kept an eye on Mlle Violette, hoping she wouldn't be sick. I was in no mood to talk. James must have sensed my tension because he didn't seek to make conversation either.

At the hotel, bellboys rushed to our assistance as we made our way up the steps. Mlle Violette now struggled to stand upright and walk. When we got to the atrium, we were met by M. Francois. He took charge and promised to lead Mlle Violette to her room.

"Thank you for your help tonight," I said to James. I felt awkward in his company.

"Always at your service," he answered.

"Well," I said and motioned to the lift. He walked with me and waited by my side in silence. But when the lift arrived, he didn't get in with me.

"Good night, Lady Caroline," he said with a slight bow and nodded to the lift attendant to slide the doors closed.

"Good night," I answered, confused as to why he didn't get in the lift with me.

Infuriating man.

CHAPTER 12

The next morning, a casual observer loitering at the entrance of Hotel Paradis would have witnessed Lady Caroline and her Uncle Albert climbing into the back seats of a snazzy car waiting at the entrance and departing the hotel for a drive down the coast. By all indications—her enormous straw hat and beach pajamas, his old-fashioned parasol and slightly out-of-character seersucker suit, and their generous picnic basket— they were on their way to the beach.

At the same time, a young errands-boy departed from the back of the hotel on a bicycle, undoubtedly to run an errand.

If any hotel guest had then proceeded to follow Lady Caroline and Uncle Albert, they would have observed them spending the day at a secluded beach near Cap Ferrat. Him—under an umbrella, reading, sweating profusely in his suit; her— tanning, but keeping her face shaded with her enormous hat. The more astute observers, and members of the Royal Society for Natural History Appreciation, would have wondered why uncle and niece were not out searching for the elusive something-or-other orchid.

This was the nature of the thoughts that amused me as I peddled—dressed in the guise of a boy—along one of the Les Corniches, the cliff-top roads running along the Cote d'Azur. As I clung to the sharp turns and hoped not to be swept off my bicycle by a passing car, I was looking for a good and secluded spot to stash the bike and begin my hunt for the blasted orchid.

Clearing a particularly tricky corner, I gave a silent thanks to Frau Baumgartnerhoff, who, among other unorthodox ladies' accomplishments, had taught her impressionable charges how to ride bicycles along narrow and curving mountain roads in Switzerland. The skill was coming in uncommonly useful as I hugged another turn with the dexterity of a Giro d'Italia contestant. Or since I was in France, perhaps a reference to the Tour de France was more in tune. Regardless, I was enjoying my bicycle ride through the French countryside.

As my legs pumped, I congratulated myself on a well-executed morning subterfuge. Prior to dashing off to dinner and casino the previous evening, I had convinced my uncle to take part in a little charade. He was to spend the day at the beach with a hotel maid dressed like Lady Caroline—and here I was assisted by M. Francois, and a few bills to the maid—while 'the real' I traversed the coast and surveyed the cliff under cover.

Dear Uncle Albert had protested. The idea of spending the day at the beach stretched his Victorian sensibilities to their limit. He fretted about being discovered by one of his Royal Society chums in the company of a young French maid. I assured him that her disguise was infallible and that none of the older hotel guests would ever venture on the beach. But I hoped, for my mother's sake, that our little trick would go undetected. She would not be able to live down another social faux pas. Not that my uncle would have been the first peer of the realm to ever be discovered in a compromising position with a French maid.

In the end, once I had pointed out that our little scheme was all in the name of The Golden Platypus, my uncle relented.

The reason I was riding around the countryside in disguise was so I could hunt for the orchid unfettered and unobserved. Witnessing the exchange between the messenger boy and Lord Mantelbury's secretary yesterday, and a few choice tidbits from my uncle of past ploys by various Royal Society members to get their hands on The Golden Platypus in underhanded ways, had put me on my guard.

So here I was, riding along the Corniche Inferieure, with the mountains on my left and the Mediterranean on my right, dressed in a haphazard selection of my uncle's sport attire, attempting to look inconspicuous. To achieve the errands-boy look of the moment, I was wearing Uncle Albert's golfing plus fours paired with his shooting socks, a tweed waistcoat over a tattersall shirt with the sleeves rolled up, and finished off with a tie. To lend the entire ensemble an air of authenticity, I had tucked as much of my bobbed blonde hair as I could into my uncle's golfing flat cap and pulled it down over my eyes. I was glad that my maid had at least packed a pair of sturdy country walking shoes, so I wouldn't have to wear my uncle's.

I rode around undetected, spying several times different Royal Society secretaries rambling aimlessly across the countryside. I even spotted James, but stayed true to my disguise.

The day was growing hot, and my uncle's clothes were growing uncomfortable. I must admit, I stopped several times to meditate on the blue of the Mediterranean. I hoped that by communing thus with nature, she would open up to reveal her secrets to one of her daughters. After a dry sandwich, I lay down on the warm grass, under the dappled shade of the young leaves of an ancient oak, closed my eyes and let the sounds of the waves wash over me. I woke up with a start. Alas, mother nature had not revealed her secrets to me today.

I checked my watch and realized I had to pedal homeward in haste. I had arranged to synchronize my arrival back at the hotel with that of my uncle's, and the ersatz Lady Caroline, at four o'clock.

With the mountains now on my right, the sea on my left, and the sun in my eyes, I stopped off on a hill overlooking the Mediterranean to catch my breath. The view was stunning, with the sun sparkling over the crystal blue water. Below me, the countryside undulated peacefully towards the sea, with what looked like a cemetery tucked in one corner.

As I admired the view, two figures, like mirror images of each other, left the cemetery by a low gate. I recognized Baron Tacotti and Count Karowsky, and was about to call out and wave when I remembered I was in disguise. Explaining *why* seemed like more trouble than it was worth, so I simply pedaled on.

On my way to the hotel, I mused at how perfectly Catholic it was of the Baron and the Count to visit a cemetery, and wondered what had drawn them there.

Hopping from one foot to the other, checking his pocket watch impatiently, M. Francois was clearly waiting for an important delivery by the back door of the hotel. As I slowed down my bicycle, he caught sight of me and threw his hands to heaven in an exaggerated gesture of thanks.

I threw a quick glance behind me to check if a delivery van was pulling up in my wake.

"Ah, Lady Caroline! Finally!" M. Francois exclaimed, and it became clear it was me he had been expecting.

CHAPTER 13

Confused thoughts rushed through my mind: Did M. Francois need the bicycle I had borrowed urgently? Had something happened to my uncle? Had my uncle had a sunstroke? My mother would never forgive me!

"Is it Uncle Albert? Is he well?" I asked, concerned.

"There is a bit of a misunderstanding. If you would be so kind as to change out of your disguise and meet me in my office *tute de suite*."

M. Francois took the bicycle out of my hands and, with a snap of his fingers, handed it to a boy meandering in the vicinity. Then he ushered me into the hotel and through the back stairs used by the staff. I thought he was about to accompany me to my suite, but as I looked back, he was waiting at the bottom of the stairs, his hands urging me forward, his patent-leathered feet pacing, tippy-toe, in place as though to show I needed to move faster.

Questions continued to race through my mind,

as I changed into an afternoon frock: What was the misunderstanding M. Francois had alluded to? Had someone taken offense that my uncle had gone to the beach with a maid from the hotel?

Down the lift and across the lobby, on my way to M. Francois' office, it became clear that something extraordinary had happened at the hotel while I was gone. Agitated guests stood gathered in groups, whispering, while policemen walked around looking important, throwing suspicious looks at the cowering hotel patrons.

Had something valuable been stolen this time? My mind jumped to the items I had deposited on arrival and wondered if someone had pinched the family jewels. I was particularly attached to an emerald riviere necklace, which was the only jewelry my family owned that did not exhibit the propensity to blind the Gorgons. Having escaped the break-in yesterday, I sincerely hoped the thief hadn't taken a fancy to it now.

Guests gaped shamelessly as I passed through the atrium, and I could feel their eyes on my back. The marble walls of the round hall ensured that, through the magic of physics, just like at the whispering gallery of St. Paul's, I could hear their murmurs clearly. But beyond confirming to each other that I was indeed Lady Caroline, their exchanges gave me no other clues as to what had transpired.

Upon entering M. Francois' office, I was met

with a peculiar sight. Instead of sitting behind his desk, M. Francois was standing in a corner to my right, stepping in a nervous rhythm from one foot to the other, much like he had done at the back of the hotel a few minutes earlier, and twisting his hands.

As I came in, he ushered me to an empty chair by my uncle's left side and withdrew to his corner to continue his nervous shuffle. On my uncle's right sat the maid, still wearing my straw beach hat, crying.

In contrast to her, my uncle was displaying an exemplary stiff upper lip and looking down his nose at the man behind M. Francois' desk.

I turned my attention to that man as well. Heavy-set, with greasy hair brushed in neat sideways rows, he sat uncomfortably in an ill-fitting suit. I couldn't place him. He looked like a brush salesman. But could have been an insurance peddler. I settled on the latter, given that I expected my necklace had been stolen.

But that did not quite explain why the maid was crying.

"It's about time," he said and didn't even try to hide his annoyance. Who was this man?

"What!" I piped up indignantly and threw the impertinent man an unkind look. I then glanced back at the manager for clarification, but he just shook his head and indicated that I should turn forward.

"Now, Mademoiselle," the man said, and checked a paper in front of him, "Caroline. I am the Commissary of Police, Maurice Juneau."

That made more sense, but I now liked him even less. I'd quickly learned in London that policemen had a tendency to spoil all the fun.

"You are no doubt aware, Mademoiselle,—"

"My Lady," I corrected him. I had no idea what this little performance was about, but his manner vexed me and I decided to be troublesome.

It was his turn to gawk. "What?" he barked.

"I'm not a Mademoiselle, I'm a Lady, a daughter of an Earl. When you address me, the correct form is *Lady Caroline* or *My Lady*." I felt the need to assert my place with this man.

M. Francois jumped in. "Lady Caroline is the daughter—" But the Commissary cut him off with a swipe of his hand, and the manager melted back into the wall. I had never seen M. Francois so rattled.

I clearly heard the Commissary mutter something about how the English needed their own revolution, but I pretended my French was not that good.

"In that case, *Lady* Caroline," he said, emphasizing the title, "you are in no doubt aware that Mlle Violette was found dead this morning."

"What?" I said.

This caught me off guard. I looked around

the room. But the only answer I received to my questioning look was a louder cry from the maid. I really wished she would stop. She was still wearing my silk beach pajamas and those salty tears would make the most unsightly stains.

Cressida Babcock had cried all over my cream frock at her coming out party because she had been snubbed by Maximilian Rogers during the Foxtrot, and the stains where she had availed herself on my shoulder were still there, no matter what concoctions Mary had tried in the laundry room.

The maid wiped her nose on the sleeve and I decided it was better if she kept the blasted things.

"As you were one of the last people to see her alive," the Commissary said, cutting into my thoughts of home. His tone sounded even more irritated, perhaps due to the maid's incessant crying. "You are one of our primary suspects."

That got my full attention. "What? I cried out. "No, I was not aware that Mlle Violette is dead," I protested, but the Commissary raised his hand to stop me. I wondered if he had directed traffic on the busy streets of Nice before being promoted to commissary.

"You were seen, with a young man, our other suspect, walking Mlle Violette to the hotel last night."

"Yes, I did!" I raised my voice. "She was not feeling well, and I had volunteered to bring her back from Monte Carlo." It just went to show you that no good deed went unpunished, I seethed.

"If I may," M. Francois tried to cut in again, "a doctor was call—"

"Please M. Francois, I already have your statement."

I wondered if James had been interviewed already, and whether he had been treated the same way.

I also wondered, given that I was the main suspect, what my uncle and the maid were doing in this interview with me.

"Now, you were seen leaving the hotel in disguise early this morning. And it has come to light that you involved your uncle and this hotel maid in your scheme—"

"Wait, what scheme? I interrupted. "Are you referring to The Golden Platypus?" I asked, confused. Was this about Mlle Violette dying or about me trying to find the blasted orchid undercover?

"—to get rid of incriminating evidence," he said, continuing his thought. "The golden what?" he asked, clearly taken aback.

Here M. Francois jumped in with rapid French and tried to convey in the simplest terms possible the mechanics behind the Royal Society for Natural History Appreciation's annual Golden Platypus competition. I was surprised that the manager had such a vigorous grasp on the harebrained contest and was able to expound on the intricacies of English eccentricity while keeping a straight face.

The Commissary's face, however, became increasingly contorted as he tried to follow M. Francois' logic.

"Enough," the Commissary said, when his face looked like it'd had enough gymnastics for the day. "I do not know what you are talking about. I will have one of my men look into it." He waved M. Francois back to his corner.

M. Francois stifled a groan. Undoubtedly, he distrusted the ability of the average uniformed French policeman to comprehend the singularities of the English gentry. So did I.

My uncle, meanwhile, apparently satisfied with M. Francois' account of the Royal Society, nodded approvingly at the description, and beamed at the Commissary with a beatific smile, as though the whole matter was now settled.

A shy knock on the door, and a corresponding bark from the Commissary, brought in a slight young man in a policeman's uniform, whose cap kept sliding down over his eyes.

The young man approached the Commissary, exchanged a few words in hushed tones, and handed him a small brown glass bottle. The Commissary looked at the bottle now resting in his large palm and a wide smile spread across his face.

As he looked up, I decided that if ever there

was a man who should not smile, it was the Commissary. The spreading of his fleshy lips and the bearing of his teeth, which he clearly considered a smile, contorted his visage into a grotesque caricature—his bulbous nose stretched wider and his bulging cheeks swallowed his beady eyes.

Or was his expression something other than joy?

"Lady Caroline, Sir," he began, clearly enjoying what was to come, "I had your rooms searched—"

"What!" I shot out.

He put out a hand again. "Quite within my rights, given the nature of the crime," he said, with a note of cruelty in his voice. "Mlle Violette died from a large dose of tropane alkaloids. And this bottle," he said, holding the bottle between two thick fingers for us to see, "containing the same substance, was just recovered from your uncle's suite." He paused, a satisfied grin disfiguring his face.

My uncle nodded in recognition.

"That's the one," he piped up at the most inopportune moment. "*Atropa belladonna.* Commonly known as belladonna or deadly nightshade. The beautiful, but deadly, lady," he said with a misty voice. "How exciting!"

I cast a fierce look at my uncle. He was not among his Royal Society friends. Now was not the time to exhibit his knowledge.

"Ah, so you are familiar with it?" the Commissary turned his attention to my uncle.

"Yes, quite," he beamed back.

I sank a little further into my chair. My uncle was going to get us hanged.

CHAPTER 14

Another knock broke the tension in the room. At this, a man entered the room forcefully. I turned to look and saw M. Francois visibly relax.

"Ah, M. le Juge," the manager said, glowing at the new arrival.

M. Francois launched into another rapid-fire French exchange with M. le Juge. I'd read enough French history to know that in the French judicial system, *juge d'instruction*, an Examining Magistrate, was involved in the evidence-gathering stage of investigations of suspicious deaths.

As the manager spoke, appraising the Magistrate of my mother's importance to society at large, and to the hotel in particular, and of my relation to her, I looked at the new arrival. A tall man, the Magistrate exuded a sense of calm borne out of confidence. His white hair belied a strong body with a straight back. And he was wearing a well-tailored suit, unlike the Commissary. The Magistrate was positively dapper.

The Magistrate listened to M. Francois with patience, nodded a few times, and then turned to my uncle and me. "Lord Tatham, Lady Caroline, we will not be detaining you much longer. Please, do not think that you are under any suspicion."

I heard the Commissary choke. But instead of contradicting his superior, the Commissary threw us a look that clearly indicated he wished guillotines were still the norm in France.

"M. le Juge," the Commissary said, and vacated his seat. The Magistrate sat down behind the desk and his penetrating gray eyes gazed at each of the three people seated in front of him in turn.

With one word, he dismissed the maid, whose cries and hiccups had measured out the passing minutes. Realizing she was free to go, her cries turned to a loud wail as the manager showed her out of the room.

"Lord Tatham," the magistrate addressed my uncle, "I'm Henri De Rochard, the Examining Magistrate for this case." His poise and manners had hinted at an aristocratic background, and his name affirmed it. "I'm afraid we will need to hold on to your bottle of belladonna for the moment, but as there is no other evidence against you, you are free to go. I may seek your expertise on plants at a later date."

Uncle Albert, flattered at the suggestion that his knowledge might be of use to the authorities, oh-ed and um-ed in a flustered manner, and hobbled towards the door.

The Magistrate now turned his attention to me. The Commissary was hovering in the background, but the Magistrate did not invite him to sit.

"Lady Caroline," the Magistrate said, "I shall only take a bit more of your time, as I understand you accompanied Mlle Violette back to the hotel from the casino last night."

I nodded.

"As the Commissary no doubt informed you, Mlle Violette died from an overdose of belladonna. Given the time of death, we estimate she ingested the poison at some point last night, just before or shortly after she arrived at the hotel."

I nodded again. But then something he'd said caught my attention. "You mean there is a possibility she took the poison herself?" I said.

"The doctor has confirmed that she died of an atropine overdose. But whether it was administered by someone else, in her drink at the casino, for example, or she ingested it herself, we are not certain at this time. She had belladonna in her room. I believe dancers in Paris still employ the substance to enhance their appearance."

From the corner of my eye I could see the Commissary wince, no doubt finding it painful that the Magistrate was so forthcoming with information.

My mind jumped to the stolen letter, and I wondered if Mlle Violette could really have committed suicide over its disappearance.

"What can you recall about Mlle Violette's behavior last night?"

The events were fresh in my mind. "Well, she looked quite intoxicated by the end of the night. That is why I offered to take her back to the hotel," I said.

"Did none of the gentlemen volunteer?" the Magistrate asked with a raised eyebrow.

"I believe all gentlemen were otherwise occupied," I answered with delicacy.

"You said Mlle Violette looked intoxicated. Did you see her consume alcohol?"

I thought back to the previous night. Mlle Violette did not lack for drinks or company the whole night. With Mlle Violette's current benefactor, Lord Withermorlington, away on business, the role was most willingly fulfilled by Baron Tacotti, Count Karowsky, M. Arnold, even some of the secretaries of the Royal Society. I related all that to the Magistrate.

Before the Magistrate could proceed with the interview, a question popped up in my mind. "What taste does belladonna have?"

"Bitter. Why do you ask?"

"Well, if Mlle Violette was poisoned at the casino, wouldn't she have tasted the poison in her drink?"

"With the popularity of cocktails nowadays,"

the Magistrate said, "gin could have easily masked the taste, or tonic water, for example."

I nodded and thought back again to the previous night.

The Magistrate leaned back in his chair and studied me. "Is something troubling you?" he asked.

"Well, it's just that," I began, unsure what the Magistrate would think of my comment, "as you say, cocktails are popular nowadays...and each type of cocktail is served in a uniquely shaped glass..." I thought back to all the drinks Mlle Violette had received from gentlemen during the night. "So, I can recall with some exactitude what cocktails Mlle Violette consumed." I listed them off on my fingers. "A cocktail glass of martini, a rocks glass of gin and tonic, a coupe of Soixante-Quinze, and a Collins glass of Singapore Sling, among some flutes of champagne."

The list surprised me. At the time, I had thought Mlle Violette's consumption excessive, but had not realized exactly how much she had put away.

I looked up at the Magistrate, who was looking at me, his brow furrowed. He had joined his hands at the fingertips, as though thinking.

While I waited for him to speak, I thought about my chum Edwina Thomson-Brown, who'd had one too many Bee's Knees and was sick all over Clementine Westley's Aubusson rug at Bloxam

House two summers ago. And although Edwina proclaimed she felt like dying the next morning, in essence, she did not.

When the Commissary first said that Mlle Violette had died during the night, I assumed she had died from excessive drinking. But it appeared that, like in the case of Edwina Thomson-Brown, alcohol hadn't killed Mlle Violette either.

I thought about Mlle Violette's behavior last night. What I had assumed were signs of intoxication were actually symptoms of poisoning. I shuddered. Poison must have been slipped into one of the drinks. But which one, and by who?

"Did you see anyone put anything in one of Mlle Violette's drinks?" the Magistrate asked as though he had read my mind.

I shook my head. With so many men in dinner jackets milling about, carrying glasses, and with Poppy bending my ear about some dashing foreign prince or other, dividing my attention, it was hard to know exactly who had poisoned Mlle Violette's drink.

The Magistrate was about to dismiss me when the incident with Mlle Rosalie stood out in my mind. "There was a disturbance caused by Mlle Rosalie's arrival," I said. "Someone could have handed Mlle Violette a poisoned drink during the confusion." I proceeded to relate the event with Mlle Rosalie to the Magistrate. He asked if I remembered which gentleman handed out drinks at that point. But the only thing I could clearly remember was that Count Karowsky led Mlle Rosalie away from the scene, and Baron Tacotti stayed by Mlle Violette's side.

As I left, I recalled it was shortly after the incident with Mlle Rosalie that Mlle Violette had started losing her sparkle.

CHAPTER 15

Thus freed from the police interview, I rushed to my uncle's suite.

"Uncle Albert!" I breezed into his rooms. "What is this about the police finding poison in your room?"

My uncle looked up unhurriedly from the botanical book in his lap. While I had been chatting to the Magistrate, he had managed to change into his velvet smoking jacket, had his foot up on the stool, and a glass of sherry by his elbow.

"Ah, my child," he said, as though surprised to see me, "come in, come in." He waved me into the room. I was not entirely sure he had heard me ask about the poison.

"But the poison, uncle, what of the poison?"

Wilford cleared his throat. "If you permit me, My Lady," he said, from his position by the door, "I may be able to elucidate the matter."

I nodded.

"It seems the Commissary accused your uncle prematurely."

"You mean Uncle Albert did not have the poison?"

"Not quite," the old valet said and cast his eyes down. "However," he continued, looking a bit more confident, "it seems the police, after conducting a thorough search of the hotel, removed medicines and tonics from more than one guest's room containing atropine. I am given to understand that they have collected a surprisingly large selection of medicinal compounds containing the poison. Your uncle is, fortuitously, only one of many in possession of the deadly substance. The ubiquity of the poison has caused quite a conundrum among the police. And it removes the specter of suspicion hanging over your uncle."

"Really?" I found this new information quite intriguing. But my uncle still hadn't explained why he was in possession of such a poisonous ingredient. "I still don't understand why you happen to have it? Have you been using it for your eyes?" I knew in centuries past women used belladonna to make their eyes appear more attractive, but couldn't fathom why my uncle should.

"Oh, no," my uncle said and chuckled. "It's for the gout, my dear. It reduces the pain somewhat."

I nodded. That was a more reasonable explanation. But I was still confused. Was there an outbreak of gout among the guests of the hotel?

"What about all the other bottles the police

collected? I thought it went out of fashion centuries ago!" I said.

"Come, my dear. Sit by me. I think once you know more about the flower, you'll understand its power."

He gazed at the book in his lap and I sat next to him. The book was opened to a page of a purple flower with jet black berries.

"The belladonna," my uncle said, running his arthritic fingers over the illustration on the page "with its magnificent purple flowers and shiny black berries, is a fascinating plant. Its Latin name is *Atropa belladonna*—named after one of the three Fates, Atropos. How is your Greek Mythology? The three fates: Clotho, who spins the thread of life, Lachesis, who measures its length, and Atropos, who cuts the string. How appropriate and how poetic. Never was a plant more aptly named, because belladonna, used improperly, truly cuts one's life short."

"But if it's so deadly, why would so many people at the hotel have it in their possession?" I cut his rambling short.

"Ah, now, that is a good question. It's been used for centuries to cure many ailments and to ease pain. Even Shakespeare used it on his Juliet for her death-like slumber. But it's an imprecise medicine, with unpredictable effects. And one would be a fool to trifle with it." He turned to his man. "Who did you say had belladonna removed from their suites, Wilford?"

"If my sources are accurate, Lord Abington uses a belladonna tincture as a cold and hay-fever remedy, Lord Fetherly treats a nervous colon, flatulence and indigestion with a belladonna tonic, and Lord Mantelbury, who likes his drink, was sent by Lady Mantelbury to a dubious doctor in the United States, who uses belladonna as a cure for alcoholism. Lord Mantelbury carries a bottle of the stuff with him, just in case Lady Mantelbury does a personal search. And Lord Packenham uses the substance as a muscle relaxant and pain relief for an old hunting injury."

"Pffh! Hunting injury! He fell off his horse, more like," my uncle interjected.

We sat in silence, Uncle Albert smirking and sipping his sherry, no doubt thinking of Lord Packenham's fall. I, in turn, was endeavoring to forget the ailments of the members of the Royal Society.

"Tell me, Carol," my uncle finally spoke up, "what was the young woman like last night? How did she act?"

I shuddered, unsure if I wanted to go into such detail. But my uncle was looking eagerly into my face, waiting for me to reply. "Well," I began tentatively, "to me, she seemed like she'd had a bit too much to drink. She had consumed so many cocktails at the casino. She was disoriented, weak, and couldn't walk."

My uncle nodded. "Ah, what a pity," he said, gazing in the distance. "I would have wished to see the poison's effect first-hand. Consider yourself lucky."

I stared at my uncle. I couldn't find the right words to chastise him.

"But what of the orchid, my girl? What of the orchid? Have you located it?"

My uncle's mind worked in mysterious ways.

"Not quite," I said. "I saw the bumblebee a few times," I said.

Or at least I thought I did. I had no idea how to tell the flat-winged bumblebee from any other. The illustrations in my uncle's books were all well and good, but out in the open, one stinging insect looked much like another.

"But no sighting of the flowers themselves," I said, delivering a visible blow to him.

The light in his eyes dimmed, and my uncle sank back in his seat, crestfallen.

"Speaking of sightings, though," I continued, seeking to raise his spirits, "I did see the other secretaries out and about. I don't think any of them recognized me. So it seems as though we are all still on the lookout. No one has discovered the orchid yet."

Uncle Albert nodded and smiled feebly, but I could tell this did not encourage him greatly.

"Although, I thought it was strange that I saw

Count Karowsky," I said, remembering, "in the company of Baron Tacotti, out on the cliffs as well. I thought nothing of it at first, but now I wonder if he was also out looking for the flower."

"Oho! What is the sly young man up to, I wonder?" Uncle Albert said, perking up.

"I thought you said he wasn't going to try and compete for the prize."

"So I did, so I did," my uncle replied pensively. "Where did you see him, exactly?"

"At a small cemetery overlooking the sea. An odd place for a cemetery, I thought. But I guess with a great eternal view."

"Interesting," he said, almost to himself. "The soil would be a tad rich...they prefer altogether a more chalky, sandy soil...but I wonder what the devil he is up to..."

I shuddered slightly at my uncle's reference to the richness of the soil, but wondered what he was on about. "What is it?" I said, intrigued.

"Well, now, it's curious. I would not expect the orchid to grow in a graveyard, but Count Karowsky is a preeminent flower man. The Dutch know their way around flowers." I wanted to correct him about Count Karowsky's nationality, but it would not have made a difference. Uncle was correct on one point—Poppy had said the Count had become extremely rich over the past few years from his flower breeding and greenhouses. "Maybe he knows something I don't," my uncle concluded.

He looked up at me, the sparkle back in his eyes. "Young Carol, I would like you to go investigate that cemetery and report back to me tomorrow."

I wrinkled my nose. "Must I prod with the stick?" I asked without hope.

"Most definitely," my uncle nodded vigorously.

I caught a movement out of the corner of my eye and looked just in time to see Wilford trying to suppress a snigger. I could not fault him, though. If the job hadn't fallen in my lot, I would have found the whole thing extremely diverting as well.

CHAPTER 16

While I had fortuitously avoided afternoon tea, and the accompanying glances and gossip, detained, as it were, in the manager's office, I could not avoid dinner. Not after I had received a pointed invitation from Poppy. She had reverted to her Head Girl tone and had put it in no uncertain terms that I would be sorry if I missed dinner. I vaguely wondered if she could place me in detention here, where she had no authority over me.

On second thought, I decided not to try her, and dressed carefully for dinner. If one was to be the object of everyone's glances and the subject of their conversations, one had to dress her best.

I was, after all, the person who had accompanied Mlle Violette back to the hotel last night, and was acutely aware that such a confluence of events was rich fodder for rumors.

One benefit of being suspected of murder was that people left one well alone. Nowhere was that more beneficial than in my relations with Lady Morton.

As I walked into the dining room, I could sense that Lady Morton was at a crossroads. She was probably dying to speak to me, to hear more about my police interview, but good breeding prevented her from seeking the society of a suspected murderess. And even if she didn't truly believe me capable of murder, the mere taint of being so closely associated with one tempered some of her enthusiasm towards me.

I could only hope that this temperance would abate her threat to unite me with Cecil.

"Are you not concerned about your reputation by being seen with me?" I teased Poppy as I sat down at her table.

"Don't be an ass," Poppy retorted with aplomb. "I know you to be enough of a pushover to swallow poison rather than to give it to someone. No one who knows you could suspect you of being a murderess."

I wondered if what she said was true, but didn't dwell on it.

"Lady Morton seems to think me capable," I said.

"She's resentful because the attention is not on her. I'm sure she's searching for a way to bring the hotel's attention back to herself."

"Was it ever?"

"No, not really, but in her mind."

"She could always congratulate herself on preventing a ruinous union between Cecil and a suspected murderess," I suggested.

"Ah, but that would not have the desired effect. She doesn't really suspect you, she is just putting on airs. She would never jeopardize Cecil's chance to marry into your family—"

"Which is nil, I should hope, but for my mother," I interjected.

"—by publicly acknowledging you as a suspected murderess," Poppy continued, finishing her thought.

"But enough of Lady Morton and Cecil," I pleaded, "what say the wagging tongues about Mlle Violette's death? Is it now generally known that Mlle Violette was poisoned?"

Being out all day and then in the manager's office, I had been deprived of the latest gossip.

"Oh, quite!," Poppy said. "Most of the hotel suspects Mlle Rosalie. The theory goes that with Mlle Violette out of the way, Mlle Rosalie hoped to get back in Lord Withermorlington's favor and finish her villa. But the irony of it is that Lord Withermorlington seems to have acquired a new lover in Paris."

"What? Already?" I couldn't quite believe that Lord Withermorlington would be so callous.

"Rumor has it, Mlle Violette had made her way to the Riviera after an argument with Lord Withermorlington, hoping that he would follow her and make a grand gesture of some kind to reconcile. In a way, Lord Withermorlington did make a grand gesture and replaced her with a new dancer."

Now that was interesting. Could Mlle Violette, jilted by her lover, have committed suicide after all?

"What about the stolen letter?" I said, my mind jumping to the still unexplained break-in. "Does that fit into Mlle Violette's death?"

"Indeed," Poppy said, "a competing theory about Mlle Violette's death is that she was murdered over the contents of the letter."

"It could be suicide," I proposed. "Perhaps a blackmailer in possession of the letter made demands she could not meet, and she took her own life instead."

"Suicide?" Poppy retorted. "I thought the police were investigating a murder."

I nodded. It was difficult to make sense of the whole thing. Knowing so little about Mlle Violette, it was hard to formulate a theory one way or the other.

"Apparently the hotel is awash with belladonna," I said, picking up a different thread.

"Yes, I heard. Marvelous luck!"

Just then, the waiter arrived to take our orders. While Poppy was examining him on his knowledge and recall of the evening's selection, I let my mind wander over all that had transpired at the hotel.

The rivalry between Mlle Violette and Mlle Rosalie was evident, but was it enough to lead to murder? And was an unfinished villa a sufficient motive? I didn't really know.

The missing letter was another puzzle. How did the letter fit in with the murder? And what kind of criminal would take only a letter, but not jewels? Most strange.

Plus, what kind of letter could be so damming to lead to suicide, or, conversely, so valuable to lead to murder?

As the waiter stepped away, Poppy took a sip of champagne and turned to me with a frown. "I have to admit, Gassy, I spent the day thinking you the most hurtful snob, for not inviting me to the beach with your uncle," she said, sounding like a petulant child. "But once your uncle came back to the hotel with the maid, and your charade was revealed, I didn't mind so much. And now that you have been thoroughly embarrassed, I'm quite satisfied." She gave me a look that invited me to challenge her. I knew better.

Apparently, we were done discussing the murder for this evening. And perhaps rightly so.

"Would you have liked to spend the day either with my uncle or scaling the cliffs of the Cote d'Azur with me?" I said.

"No, probably not," Poppy agreed. "But I would have liked to be asked, all the same."

"So, does the whole hotel know about my little

subterfuge?"

"Oh, rather!" she exclaimed, beaming. "You should have heard Lord Packenham on the subject. Said he couldn't abide the degradation of the Royal Society. Decried the Society succumbing to social pressure. And concluded that that was what you got for allowing women into the rarefied club as secretaries."

"The scoundrel! I dare him to say it to my face," I replied, feeling the injustice deeply.

"Oh, I would not pay attention to him. From what James said, all the other members of the Royal Society know Lord Packenham to have done far more underhanded things to win that beast in the display case."

"You've spoken to James?" I said, hoping I didn't sound too eager.

"Oh, yes. He was one of the first people to be interviewed by the police, and then we spent a rather nice tea together on the terrace. He is quite a nice chap. Too bad he hasn't got a penny."

I nodded absentmindedly. It sounded like a much more agreeable way to spend the day. At least, now that my cover had been revealed, I didn't have to spend another sweltering day in heavy woolen clothing.

I mused about where James was this evening. Probably at dinner with the other secretaries. Or working late with Lord Packenham on their own schemes to win the contest. I wondered what his interview with the police had been like, and whether he was a top suspect.

"Are the members of the Society really competing for the honor of displaying that ghastly creature?" Poppy interrupted my thoughts.

I nodded and mirrored the incredulous look on her face.

"I don't suppose it's the platypus itself," I said. "I think it's more to do with the honor of winning whatever the latest harebrained competition is."

Although, considering all the calamities the trophy had suffered at various stately homes, managing to still resemble the creature it had been when living lent it a certain esteemed pedigree.

But I suspected that the contests and prizes were immaterial. For most members, the Society —and the trips undertaken in its name—was a chance to get away from the rigor imposed by their wives.

"My uncle Bartholomew," Poppy said, in a very flat and serious tone, "while at Oxford, participated in a race organized by his Young Agrarians Club. Up the Oxford Canal, from Oxford to Rugby, through Napton-on-the-Hill, with twelve geese in his boat. The chap that arrived first with all geese intact was declared a winner. Flocks of feral geese, from the ones that escaped along the racecourse, still roam Oxfordshire and Northamptonshire, they say."

I choked on my soup, laughing. A few guests

turned to stare.

Once I had recovered, I said, "I suspect the Society outdoes itself with ever more ridiculous tasks and tournaments to keep their wives at a safe distance—at home. No woman brought up on a steady diet of Victorian sensibility would ever choose to be a part of it."

"I say!" Poppy said, and now I almost dropped my soup spoon. "I have a capital idea! Tomorrow, I shall join you on your expedition. I'm rather good at country walks and hunting."

I was about to protest, but decided that some company would indeed be nice.

"James said all the secretaries were out looking for the flower. Oh, I rather wish to beat these men at their game. Show them what stern stuff women are made of."

Lord Packenham's words still rankled, and I agreed.

"Oh, it will be jolly fun!" Poppy gushed. "Plus, it will give me a chance to explore the coast for a villa location." She took another sip of champagne and her eyes came slightly unfocused. "One would have thought M. Arnold would be more forthcoming now that his star client is dead," Poppy said. I thought she was being a tad unfeeling. "But he does seem to have taken Mlle Violette's death rather badly. I can't think why," she concluded.

I left her with her thoughts of villas and vistas,

and turned my attention to the dinner.

As the waiter cleared away the ice cream bowls, Poppy pushed back her chair, and said, "Well, good night. I am off to rally us some provisions from the kitchen and secure a vehicle for tomorrow."

Poppy had assumed the air of a general working on a new plan of attack ever since deciding to join me on my expedition tomorrow. I suspected that with M. Arnold indisposed, and the villa hunt seemingly on hold, Poppy was looking for a new project to marshal.

Perhaps Poppy, given that she was christened after the goddess of spring, Persephone, would have better luck at divining the elusive orchid.

CHAPTER 17

On my way to my suite after dinner, M. Francois intercepted me in the atrium with a missive from my mother.

And while a casual observer may have assumed that the thick stack of folded pages M. Francois handed me was a letter, it was, in fact, a telegram.

To the delight of the telegraph companies on three continents and a small island in the Pacific, my mother had never learned the proper way to send a telegram, and her epistle-length communications over the wires, kept many an executive's wife in fur.

The latest installment delivered somewhat surprising news.

Distilled to its essence, the four pages of telegram warned me to stay away from the advances of any fourth sons of Earls. If I was interested in marrying into Lord Haswell's family, she would immediately arrange a nice country party, invite Viscount Otley, and the matter could be settled in mere weeks.

It was well-known among mothers with daughters of marriageable age that Viscount Otley was the courtesy title of Lord Haswell's son Leopold, who, as first-born, would one day be the 7th Earl of Haswell. What was known among the aforementioned daughters was that Leopold Haswell also happened to be a complete bore.

Leopold was over ten years my senior, and the fact that he was still available, despite being in line for a sizable title, should tell one all one needed to know. Not that he was a bad person, he was just not my cocktail of choice. Nor anyone else's, it seemed.

My mother was correct on only one point—James was the fourth son of the Earl of Haswell. But everything else contained and alluded to in her telegram was complete poppycock.

I stood stunned in the atrium, ambushed, as it were, by my mother, and wondered two things: how my mother had got word of my meetings and conversations with James, and who would read so much into their meaning.

As if answered by divine providence, Lady Morton's voice, currently engaged in accosting the poor manager's assistant, carried across the atrium.

Having thus received my answer, I decided against favoring my mother's telegram with one. But as I made my way to my suite, some stray thoughts began to solidify into a question.

Both my mother and Poppy, just now at dinner, had referred to James' financial state. Was he really that poorly off?

I thought back to my meeting with James on the day of my arrival. He had alluded to the fact that he was obliged to seek a new position after my uncle dismissed him. Now I wondered what had happened to Lord Packenham's original secretary. How had James been able to secure the position of Lord Packenham's secretary so promptly? Had Lord Packenham not had a secretary at the time? That seemed unlikely.

So the question remained, what had happened to Lord Packenham's old secretary? And also, why was James so desperate to stay in the South of France? Presumably, with his connections, he could get a position in London without much trouble.

An uncharitable thought floated to the top: was James involved in this whole affair of letters and Mlle Violette? The image of James sitting in the manager's office with the police after the robbery swam across my mind's eye. I once again wondered if he had anything to do with the robbery?

Was James a blackmailer? Impossible!

And now an even more unkind thought began to trouble me: why had James offered to help me take Mlle Violette back to the hotel? At the time, I had chalked it up to being gentlemanly. But now, I wondered why he had materialized by my side, seemingly out of thin air? Had he been watching Mlle Violette the whole night at the casino? Had he added the poison to her drink? Had he accompanied me back to the hotel in order to make certain that Mlle Violette had ingested sufficient poison to die during the night?

I told myself that I was being ridiculous, but the unpleasant thoughts continued to mount.

Shortly before falling asleep, I mused that James, as Uncle Albert's former secretary, and Lord Packenham's current one, was in a most advantageous position to steal poison from his employers.

Had James attempted to frame my uncle for Mlle Violette's death?

CHAPTER 18

Early the next morning, I realized I was sorry I had not asked Poppy to organize my search for the orchid sooner.

While the previous day I had approached the flower forage as a solitary mission, drawing upon skills imparted to me by Frau Baumgartnerhoff during a week devoted to surviving an avalanche in the Alps, Poppy had an altogether different approach to exploring the wilderness.

She tackled the search for the orchid as though organizing a safari on the planes of the Serengeti. Or at least a country house hunting party.

Having grown up in Boston, my mother eschewed hosting hunting parties. She considered it one of her few deficiencies and fretted that the lack of hunts on our estate might affect father's political career. To my mother's credit, though, her lack of understanding of hunting parties prevented her from ever attempting to host one.

Thus, I had grown up without an intimate knowledge of hunting parties. But as I had attended a few, I knew their basic structure. And it was evident, as early as breakfast, that Poppy had organized our excursion for the day like a country house hunting party.

The day began with a hearty breakfast. My Swiss muesli flakes were dismissed as inadequate, and a full English breakfast was served.

Then we drove down the coast and after a while stopped off for a spot of lunch.

During our excursion, two cars had been escorting us. The first one conveyed us to various bluffs and hills to conduct our flower search, the second was laden with a tent, chairs, a small table, and several baskets of food and drinks. These were now set, spread out, and erected, and Poppy and I had lunch under the shade of a marquee, on a table with a proper tablecloth, cutlery, china and crystal. We gazed at the blue sea while welcoming its breeze.

Lunch was followed by a brief rest and some drinks. And in the early afternoon we played a game of badminton. Although I much preferred tennis, I consented to play Poppy, just this once.

Poppy's mother had been a ladies' doubles champion in the All England Open Badminton Championship in 1899, and Poppy never let the pupils of Boughton Monchelsea School for Girls forget it. Poppy had been the star badminton player at school and today she showed me no mercy. As always, her game was fast, strong, and aggressive.

Thoroughly humiliated by Poppy, we took another break for refreshments. And thus the sun made its arc across the sky, and much like during a true country party, not much hunting was done.

But on the way back to the hotel, we chanced to drive by the cemetery where I had seen the Baron and the Count. I hadn't forgotten my uncle's bidding and couldn't postpone a visit to the cemetery much longer. Thus, sticks in hand, Poppy and I went to investigate.

"So your uncle thinks the orchid is here?" Poppy asked, with unmasked doubt in her voice.

"What other reason would Count Karowsky have to be here?"

We looked around. While the cemetery looked like any other, there was something different about it. And as I walked among the headstones and small mausoleums, I saw that it was a cemetery for soldiers from the great war. I knew that during the great war some hotels and villas along the coast had been turned into hospitals and sanatoriums for wounded soldiers.

I walked around in silence, thoughts of my brother flooding my mind. I realized the Baron and the Count had visited here not for the flower, but perhaps to pay respects at a friend's grave.

"Let's go, Poppy, I don't think we'll find the flower here," I said.

As we roamed along the bluffs, looking at the

vistas, my thoughts drifted again to the question of Mlle Violette's death. Something Poppy had said the previous night made me doubt some of the assumptions made about Mlle Violette.

"Poppy," I said, "you know how people said that Mlle Violette had come down here to build a villa?"

"Mmm," Poppy said, nodding absentmindedly. She was currently reclining under the patchy shade of an Aleppo pine, enjoying a glass of warm lemonade.

"Well, I wonder if that is quite correct."

"Does it matter now?" she said, sounding uninterested.

"You said Mlle Violette came down from Paris after an argument with Lord Withermorlington. What if Lord Withermorlington had withdrawn his offer for a villa? What if there never had been such an offer? Think about it. Why would he build her a villa if he was already enamored with another chorus girl?"

"As a parting gift?" she said and shrugged. "Why would she spend so much time with M. Arnold if they were not working on plans to build a villa?"

"I don't quite know. But what if the villa was just a way to hide something else?"

"What? You mean an affair?"

It was my turn to shrug. It was possible, but I was not convinced that M. Arnold was wealthy and influential enough for Mlle Violette. "The missing letter troubles me," I said after a pause. As Poppy didn't reply, I assumed the missing letter didn't trouble her, but I continued, "Why did Mlle Violette die so soon after the letter was stolen? And what was in that letter?"

"More lemonade?" was all Poppy could deliver on the subject.

I pressed on, undeterred. "What about the other part of the rumor, that Mlle Violette was down here to start a business? Why come all the way down here? Why not stay in Paris? And what was the nature of her business to be? What if she was about to establish a blackmailing enterprise?"

Poppy remained silent, and I thought she was indifferent to the topic of conversation. But after a moment she spoke up, "There might be something in this blackmail theory of yours. I heard some whisperings that before Lord Withermorlington, most of Mlle Violette's lovers were men high in government and army. British, German, French. It is conceivable that she might have been tempted to blackmail these men with compromising letters, now that she did not have the financial support of Lord Withermorlington."

"And what if M. Arnold was also involved in the scheme?" I suggested. There had to be an explanation why Mlle Violette had spent so much time in the company of M. Arnold.

"Gassy!" Poppy exclaimed. "M. Arnold is a respectable architect. Why would he need to get involved in blackmail?"

I didn't have an answer. But something in M. Arnold's devil-may-care attitude and the way he had been spending at the casino made me think he had an income greater than his proceeds from the villas.

Even if M. Arnold had not been involved in Mlle Violette's blackmail plot, I was beginning to think that the stolen letter was at the center of her death.

CHAPTER 19

I spent the evening thinking over my conversation with Poppy.

Something about Mlle Violette had grabbed hold of my imagination. If she had not come to the Riviera to build a villa, had she come to blackmail one of her old lovers? Was her target at the hotel?

The more I thought about Mlle Violette, the more I became convinced that there was more to her than the dolled-up persona she presented to the thirsting eyes of the male world. Her murder was in a way an affirmation of, if not hidden depths, then at least tantalizing secrets.

Not only had she been in the physical possession of a secret, in the form of the letter, a secret which someone broke into a hotel safe to take. But her very existence had threatened someone enough to kill her.

I wondered how someone so seemingly insignificant, a chorus girl from a Parisian cabaret music hall, could have such power over people.

Yes, I had no doubt of Mlle Violette's power over

someone, because who, except the most desperate person, one who feels powerless, one who sees no other way out, would commit murder?

My mind jumped to the question of suspects. Of course, the likeliest candidate was Mlle Rosalie. She had suffered most grievously. Mlle Violette's rise had been Mlle Rosalie's demise. Mlle Violette had usurped Mlle Rosalie's lover, social standing, and even her villa architect.

Not only that, but the ingenue had gone a step further, had shown foresight not evident in Mlle Rosalie, and had made plans for a business.

Yes, Mlle Violette was intriguing, and I wondered how I could find out more about her.

While there was plenty of gossip about her at teatime and dinner, few people had firsthand knowledge of her. Poppy was just as much in the dark about her as I was. And although I suspected that Lady Morton might know a few more details about Mlle Violette's lovers—after all, Mlle Violette had specialized in men of Lady Morton and my mother's age—I doubted the old snob would admit to knowing anything about her. And I was too timid to bring up the topic of lovers with my uncle.

What about the suspects? I wondered again. Mlle Violette had appeared drunk towards the end of the night. I now knew that she was most likely exhibiting the effects of the belladonna poison.

I gazed out of the window and at the people strolling on the promenade, letting my eyes roam over them. Who were the people around her at the casino?

Mlle Violette had not lacked for company. The entire evening, she was surrounded by various admirers—M. Arnold, Count Karowsky, Baron Tacotti, a few of the Royal Society secretaries (I really should attempt to learn their names). Even James. And there had also been a few women—the ones encircling M. Arnold and Poppy, although I didn't consider her a suspect.

And then there was Mlle Rosalie. Yes, Mlle Rosalie kept cropping up with disagreeable regularity. And as detective fiction has taught us, poison was a woman's weapon of choice.

Mlle Rosalie had certainly put something in her own drink. Had she managed to put something in Mlle Violette's drink? With no one noticing?

What if Mlle Rosalie had put on an act in order to distract—to allow the killer to poison Mlle Violette's drink while everyone was looking the other way?

But if Mlle Rosalie was guilty, why hadn't the police arrested her? She had the motive and the opportunity. Perhaps she even had a bottle of belladonna in her room, given how popular the substance was among the guests.

Yes, I concluded, Mlle Rosalie was a very suitable suspect.

Then I remembered the safe. The safe break-in and Mlle Violette's death had to be linked. Why would Mlle Rosalie steal a letter? Was the letter about her?

But Mlle Rosalie must have had an accomplice. Whoever broke into the safe was an expert. Of course, Baron Tacotti was the obvious choice for that little number.

And I had seen Baron Tacotti hand Mlle Violette drinks. But I had also seen the other gentlemen —the Count and M. Arnold—do the same. And without knowing which drink was poisoned, it was hard to know who had done it.

What about James? The point that troubled me most about James was the fact that I had seen him interviewed by the French police shortly after the hotel break-in. Did that make him guilty of the theft?

Or was there another explanation? If Mlle Violette had been here to blackmail an old lover, was it not conceivable that James' current employer, Lord Packenham, was that man?

No, that was an idiotic supposition, I told myself. But was it? Would not that explain his behavior towards me?

What if he means to warn me to stay away from him because he is a murderer and doesn't wish me to get involved? I need to stop reading romantic novels, I told myself.

I paced the room. If only there was a way to learn more about Mlle Violette and the suspects.

As I made a second unproductive round of the

suite, my gaze fell upon the discarded pages of my mother's telegram.

I had a marvelous idea.

CHAPTER 20

As horrified as my mother had been over the typing school, she was above all a practical woman. In order to lessen the social ramifications of my association with such a plebeian—at least in her mind—institution, she set out to raise the school's profile. To that end, she took it upon herself to place my classmates in respectable positions.

Now, thanks to my mother's machinations, my former schoolmates were secretaries to some of the most esteemed men of the empire. But none reached the heights of Jane, Elanor, Louisa and Philippa, my closest friends from the typing course.

Jane was secretary at the War Office, Elanor at Lloyd's, the insurance firm, and Philippa at the Bank of England. And while I had mused that a female secretary could not be installed too far up the hierarchy of the Church of England, I had been surprised just how close to the top Louisa, under my mother's urging, had been placed.

My mother's meddling had done quite a lot to

raise the profile of the secretarial school.

I summoned a messenger boy and instructed him to send four telegrams to London. I didn't know what I was looking for, but I hoped some venerable British institution or other would have a record of one of Mlle Violette's lovers. If Poppy's information was accurate, and it usually was, the pinnacles of government and army were littered with the Parisian dancer's lovers.

The telegrams were simple, if a tad long. I asked my chums in high places to search for records on my suspects from the casino—Baron Tacotti, Count Karowsky, M. Arnold, Mlle Rosalie, and Mlle Violette herself—and her lover Lord Withermorlington. I hesitated whether to add Lord Packenham's name to the list, but decided against it. There was no reason for me to suspect that he had been her lover. I did, however, add a strong hint that Mlle Violette had favored relations with men in power during the war.

The messenger boy sent me a dubious look, and I realized that perhaps, on the matter of telegrams, I was not so different from my mother after all. I dismissed the thought with a shiver.

A telegram was waiting for me at breakfast. Jane, from the War Office, confirmed receipt and assured me that all of the ladies were on the case.

I didn't expect answers from my friends right away. After all, they needed time to go through records. But, just in case, I spent the day idling around the hotel and answering my uncle's correspondence.

It wasn't until tea time that my patience was rewarded. I observed a messenger boy come out on the terrace. He clutched a white piece of paper in his hands. I watched his progress with interest. Secretly, I was hoping he had a message for me. The boy scanned the tables on the terrace. I saw the confusion in his eyes. The terrace was bestrewed with ladies in elaborate sun hats and white dresses. When the head waiter pointed him in my direction, my heart began to beat a bit faster.

As I dropped a few coins into the boy's hand, however, and spied the message in his hand, my excitement ebbed.

The note contained a single line. Even without reading it, I knew I was in for a disappointment. A single line could not contain all the information I was hoping my friends would uncover. A single line could surely mean only one thing—there was no information about the suspects, Mlle Violette, or her lovers.

I took the message from the boy's hand and was about to toss it aside with a sigh, but as my eyes glided over the actual text, my heart leaped back into action. The message was again from Jane and said: "Letter by Blue Train."

My abrupt departure from the terrace raised more than a few eyebrows. I could not contain my excitement and rushed to my room to think things over. A letter meant that they had found something either too sensitive to put in a telegram, or there was too much information to send over the wires.

Either way, the single sentence ignited a fire of curiosity that I found hard to contain.

The next day, I wondered if I should meet The Blue Train, but decided I might draw too much attention to myself. After all, a killer was lurking in the hotel.

Instead, I spent the morning, and my nervous energy, walking the bluffs by the sea. Walking, stick in hand, I prodded at flowers without paying the slightest attention to them. My mind was racing as fast as The Blue Train. In my mind, I followed the train's progress down from Paris, through Dijon, Lyon and Marseille, making a sharp turn at Toulon to reach Nice in the late morning. What secrets had my friends uncovered? What mysteries had been hidden under Mlle Violette's layers of lace and makeup?

Deciding that I had given unsuspecting flat-winged bumblebees enough exercise for the morning, I headed for the hotel, where I was met by the concierge and a gratifyingly thick envelope.

I rushed to my room by the back stairs, seeking to avoid anyone who might detain me with an offer of lunch, and thus keep me from reading the letter. The maids I met on the stairs stepped aside and gave me curious looks. I mused vaguely what diversion my actions must give the employees of the hotel—a suspected murderess, fond of wearing men's clothes, and in the habit of using servants' stairs.

Barring myself in my room, I willed my hands to still long enough to open the letter.

As I began to read, my hands resumed their tremble. Now I was getting somewhere. No wonder Mlle Violette was dead.

I looked wildly around my room. Did anyone else know? Surely her killer knew.

I needed to share my findings with someone, but I didn't know who. I wondered if I should speak to the French police, but on reflection decided not to. The Commissary would resent the meddling of the upper class and take it as an affront to the working classes. And the Magistrate, who I suspected was socially well connected, might know some people mentioned in Jane's letter. Plus, he might ask how I had come to have the information. I preferred no to get my chums in London in trouble so early in their careers.

If the French police were worth their salt, they could easily get the same information.

I considered confiding in Poppy, but as M. Arnold had apparently recovered from the loss of Mlle Violette's company, Poppy was redoubling her efforts of finding a suitable site for a villa. So while all I had to look forward to was spending sweltering days, with an unforgiving sun beating down my back, tracking insufferable bees and flowers, she was whizzing up and down the coast basking in the golden rays of the Cote d'Azur, in the company of the charming architect.

In lieu of a confidant, I took a bar of Toblerone from my desk and sat down on a chaise by the window to read. Smoothing out the pages on my lap, I took a piece of triangular chocolate. Chocolate helped me think, I told myself. Plus, having now missed lunch, the candy bar would have to suffice until tea time.

Having read the letter at speed the first time, I now took the time to peruse it with care and grasp its full meaning.

The letter began with the most surprising news—Mlle Violette was well known to the War Office, and not just for her affairs with high-ranking officials. During the war, she had been a double agent. She had provided information to the British, but was suspected of providing information to the Germans as well. MI5 paid her the handsome sum of £50 a week for information. The payments had ceased after the war.

The news astonished me. I looked up from

the letter. I had no idea how Jane had procured this information. It seemed to me that it would be classified. Perhaps the newspapers had been correct when they reported that funding for the War Office and MI5—both considered extraneous since the end of the great war—had been slashed dramatically in recent years.

Perhaps the records were easier to access as a consequence of staff reductions. Or perhaps Jane, the personification of an English rose—plump lips, flushed cheeks and dewy complexion, made only more irresistible by a pair of enormous blue eyes —had charmed her way to the records. I smiled at the thought of such subversion and made a mental note to ask her about it when back in London.

I read on. Mlle Violette had a talent not only for dancing but also for befriending men of high standing in the army and government. Jane had thoughtfully attached a list of known and suspected lovers, which made me blush.

The letter went on to say that Mlle Violette's success in obtaining information from her lovers did not rest solely on her charms. She had acquired the most sensitive of documents by breaking into safes. And while I had begun to think of Mlle Violette as a wonder of nature—celebrated dancer, admired coquet, tireless lover, and now a master MI5 agent—my friend quelled my misgivings by going on to say that an accomplice, skilled in safe-breaking, was suspected.

I stared down in horror at my lap. The Toblerone wrapper was empty. I had consumed the whole thing while reading the letter.

The letter was proving to be a matter that could not be dealt with in a single Toblerone bar. A walk in the gardens was called for. The rooms were too small to contain my wild thoughts. I needed the expanse of nature to quell my mind.

CHAPTER 21

Walking the garden paths, the letter burning a hole in the pocket of my coat, my mind raced over the new facts.

While I had dismissed Mlle Violette as a crumpet, she had been involved in perilous espionage. I wondered how many other people had failed to appreciate her hidden talents.

At the bottom of the garden was a labyrinth made from tall boxwood. I could never resist a maze and headed in its direction. As I entered it and began walking its winding paths, I gathered my thoughts.

It all made sense now—the hotel safe's break-in and even Mlle Violette's death. She had been a secret agent during the war. A double agent. The secrets she shared with our own government, and the Germans, possibly saved countless lives, but also endangered many more. Who could say what secrets she revealed and whom she hurt?

In light of this new information, the most likely suspects now were her former lovers—generals, majors, captains, lieutenants. Had she stolen one secret too many? Had her past caught up with her? Had she caused someone's death and now paid for it with her life?

Perhaps the answer lay in whatever was taken from the safe. Had the letter been something to do with the war? Some old war secret? Evidence of her role as a secret agent?

As much as the letter from Jane helped throw new light on the question of Mlle Violette's death, it also gave rise to many more. Somehow, knowing more did not take me closer to the truth.

Did this mean that Mlle Rosalie was not involved in Mlle Violette's murder? But what if Mlle Rosalie had been a secret agent during the war as well? Jane's letter had included no information about Mlle Rosalie or any of my other suspects. But I couldn't be sure why that was. Had Jane been unable to find particulars on any of them? Or had she rushed to send me the sensational information about Mlle Violette? I needed to ask Jane to find out more.

But now my mind latched onto another tantalizing piece of information contained in Jane's letter—the safe break-ins. That a safe break-in also happened at the hotel could not be a coincidence. Was Mlle Violette's wartime accomplice here at the hotel? My mind jumped to Baron Tacotti. Was he not rumored to be a jewel thief?

For a moment I thought I'd had too much sun and chocolate, because I heard Baron Tacotti's voice.

His words, spoken softly, stopped me in my tracks.

"The murder complicates matters, wouldn't you agree?" he said, and I could now hear the hiss of the tip of his cigarette as he took a deep drag. He was just on the other side of the labyrinth's green wall. I stilled my breath. He exhaled. "I only agreed to the safe."

The other person's answer was too faint for me to hear. The voice was male, though.

But I heard Baron Tacotti's answer clearly enough. "I will keep what I know quiet. You have nothing to fear on that account." He paused and took another drag from his cigarette. "In deference to our friendship, be that what it may," he said as he exhaled the smoke. "And considering your help in Bad Ragaz," he added. "But if the police come after me," he continued, his tone darkening, "I will be straight with them. And don't try any funny business. My lawyer in Zurich is already in possession of my sealed statement. Life insurance policy, you see." Here the Baron paused and the other person replied, but again I couldn't hear what was said. "Let us go back," the Baron said to his companion and the crunch of footsteps on the gravel moved towards the hotel.

I had to fight my curiosity to look through the

hedge. I wanted to see who the Baron had been speaking to, but I preferred not to reveal myself to a potential killer.

Thus, I lingered in the labyrinth long enough to let the speakers get back inside the hotel.

Deciding that, by now, the two men were well away from the garden, I walked back up the terraces to the hotel, but as I entered through the French doors, I ran into James.

"James!" I exclaimed. "What are you doing here?" My heart began racing uncontrollably. Was it fright? I hoped James could not hear the loud thumps. Was he the unknown man Baron Tacotti had been speaking to in the garden?

"Hello Caroline," he replied, and for the first time since I'd arrived on the Riviera, his attitude towards me seemed less guarded. "What is it? You look flushed." He stepped towards me, and reached as though to grab my arm, but seemed to falter at the last moment. He searched my face, his crystal clear blue eyes gliding over my skin. What was he looking for?

I searched his face back, looking for any hint whether he had been the second man in the garden.

"Has something happened, Caroline?" James looked over my shoulder and into the garden.

I shook my head. I couldn't tell him about the letter and about the conversation I had just overheard. Not when I didn't know whether I could trust him. "No, everything is fine," I said, and swallowed a hard lump in my throat.

Sidestepping him, I half-expected him to block my way and ask more questions. But he didn't.

I ran confused, ready to cry, to my room. I may have used the servants' stairwell again.

CHAPTER 22

As tears blurred my vision, I stumbled into my room. I threw myself on the chaise and let the tears roll down my face freely. What had James been doing by the garden doors? I did not want to believe that he had been the second person in the garden. I was thoroughly confused.

With concerted effort, I brought my sobbing hiccups under control. Crying would not do. I sat up on the chaise and attempted to rein in my thoughts. As I found thinking about James too painful, I instead turned my attention to what I had just heard in the garden.

Could Baron Tacotti be both the thief and the murderer?

But during the war, he surely would have been at school in Switzerland. Could he also have been a spy in Paris at the same time? Or had he lied to me about Switzerland? Yet, there was so much truth in the way he described his experience at boarding school. I wondered if Frau Baumgartnerhoff might be able to find some information about him. Did headmistresses and headmasters share information readily? I laid that thought to the side.

My thoughts drifted back to James. But now I found I could think about him quite clearly, without crying. Where did he fit in? Was he Baron Tacotti's accomplice from the garden? Had he been Mlle Violette's lover during the war as well? Did he have something to hide?

As my thoughts spiraled and my mood became darker and more desperate, I decided it must be time for tea. Having skipped lunch, I wasn't about to miss out on the next meal. Plus, Poppy was bound to have some diverting news of her days spent in the company of M. Arnold.

But as I made my way to tea, I noticed that the patrons on the terrace had settled around, as though at a theater, in expectation of the premier of a new drama. I followed the direction of everyone's gaze to a table for two, occupied by a severe looking older gentleman. Based on his stiff manners, and an even stiffer collar, I assumed he was an Englishman. The man's only distinguishing feature was a narrow mustache which had managed to wedge itself under a prolonged nose. Looking down his nose, he stoically ignored all the glances in his direction.

The same could not be said of his companion. Her eyes danced across the audience on the terrace, and each time she batted her lashes, the rather large feather sticking out of her hat—a flourish better suited for the first day of Ascot than afternoon tea—fluttered in unison.

"Hello, Poppy!" I said, joining her table. As Poppy had taken the dress circle position on the terrasse, I had to sit with my back to the new couple. It suited me fine. I could quiz Poppy without the fear of being overheard. "Who is the new exotic bird and her handler?"

"That," Poppy said, and took a painfully long pause, "is Lord Withermorlington. And Gigi, the young woman by his side, is his latest ingenue from the Paris chorus line."

I stifled a little groan. I wondered how the esteemed dance establishment in Paris could keep up with Lord Withermorlington's appetite. "What is he doing here? I mean, what is he doing here with his new mistress? So soon after Violette's death. Has he no decency?"

"No," Poppy said matter-of-factly, "rumor is he doesn't. But apparently he made his way down here for Violette's funeral."

I shook my head. "How ghastly!"

As Poppy's attention was momentarily diverted by this afternoon's selection of pastries, I thought more about Mlle Violette. When I had heard that Lord Withermorlington was in possession of a new mistress, I had wondered whether Mlle Violette could have taken her own life. But the new information I had about her—a double agent and a brazen thief of war secrets—did not conform with the type of person who would commit suicide. Murder, yes, but not suicide.

As we tucked into tea, it transpired that Poppy was not concerned with Mlle Violette or Lord Withermorlington, and that her mind was occupied solely with her, so far, fruitless search for a villa.

She described the coves, bluffs, and cliffs they had visited that day, the Belle Epoque villas in need of modernization, and the old shacks that needed to be razed to the ground. She lamented that most of the prime spots were either already occupied by Russian emigres or had recently been snatched up by American parvenus.

In addition to the disappointment with the villas, it seemed that M. Arnold's heart just didn't seem to be invested in the search.

My mind jumped to M. Arnold at the casino a few nights ago. "Perhaps he is spending faster than he can build villas?" I suggested. "I mean, just look at the way he was spending at the gambling tables in Monte Carlo." *It was as if the money was not his*, but I kept that thought to myself.

"He is quite successful," Poppy said in a defensive tone, as though I had attacked M. Arnold's professional capacity. "I don't think he needs to worry about such trifles. And from what Count Karowsky said today—he joined us on a visit to a particularly dilapidated villa, with a grand garden—M. Arnold gets little gifts from his lady clients to smooth over shortages whenever luck has been against him at the tables." I had been a witness to that. Poppy sighed and looked dreamily into the distance. I wondered if she wished to give M. Arnold little gifts as well. Her father would never stand for it. "They are both so charming, don't you think?" She sighed again. "I don't know what I would do if both of them proposed to me."

"What?" I started. Was there a question of any such threat from either of them?

I wanted to warn Poppy that any attentiveness they showed towards her was not genuine; charm was part of the business etiquette of these men. Happy clients tended to open their purses wider. I worried Poppy would let herself be taken advantage of and set about to caution her. But on second thought, I decided she would not take kindly to any such warnings and might even take offense. Plus, I was certain Papa Kettering, a decorated veteran of the Boer War, would deal decisively with any interlopers.

The scrape of chair legs against the flagstones of the terrace, coupled with the renewed animation of the audience, signaled that the afternoon's performance was at an end. I turned to see Lord Withermorlington and Mlle Gigi leaving and wondered if I had missed a good show.

CHAPTER 23

While the appearance of Lord Withermorlington with Mlle Gigi perched on his arm the previous afternoon had caused a stir, it was nothing to the tsunami that ripped through the breakfast room the next morning—M. Arnold was dead.

Poppy, who enjoyed taking brisk, healthful walks in the morning, had been one of the first guests to hear the news.

"Oh, it was ghastly. Absolutely ghastly," she said, as I joined her at the table. I was rather anxious for her at first, but she kept a stiff upper lip that would do her father proud. "It was M. Francois who delivered the news to me. The police had arrived while I was taking the air. M. Francois thought I should be the first to know, given that I had an appointment with M. Arnold later today. Oh, Caroline, what am I going to do?" She almost sobbed. I worried that Poppy might have formed an attachment to M. Arnold. "Who is going to build my villa now?" she finally said. I needn't have worried.

A shadow moved across our breakfast, like a dark cloud, and I looked up to see that Lady Morton had approached our table.

"Lady Caroline, Miss Kettering-Thrapston," she said, turning to each of us with exaggerated solemnity. "May I join you for breakfast?"

Decorum prevented one from answering truthfully, but Lady Morton's sudden interest in our little company vexed me. I would have liked to remind her I was still a murder suspect, and that Poppy, having formed a close working relationship with M. Arnold, was probably a suspect in his death. But that reminded me, I knew nothing about the cause of M. Arnold's death.

I nodded to Lady Morton, and while she took her seat, I turned to Poppy. "What did the police say? How did M. Arnold die? Was it murder?"

"Oh, yes, dear," Lady Morton joined in, "do tell us all the details." Ah, now it came out! The reason Lady Morton had condescended to join us.

Poppy stiffened her back. "M. Arnold met his end at some point last evening. He had been walking the cliffs along the coast, when he must have slipped and fallen into the sea below. Some fishermen found his body on the rocks below early this morning."

"So it was an accident?" I said.

"It seems likely," Poppy answered. She paused and then added, "I would hate to think that M. Arnold met his end while looking for the ideal location for my villa." But the misty look that glazed her eyes betrayed her. I suspected Poppy found it quite romantic to think that M. Arnold had died in the pursuit of the perfect villa for her.

"Oh, these cliffs are so treacherous," Lady Morton added. "If it were up to me, I would have formed a committee to ensure each of these cliffs is secured with a solid fence. I am quite a proficient committee member. In fact…"

I let Lady Morton drone on about cottages, boats, beaches, and boardwalks in Poole, or Lyme Regis, or some other such place, while I sipped my tea and turned over the news about M. Arnold in my mind.

M. Arnold's death might very well have been an accident. But seen in the light of the break-in at the hotel, and then Mlle Violette's murder, it didn't seem likely. I wished Lady Morton had not joined us. I preferred not to discuss such matters in front of her.

So I continued to sip my tea. What connected the two deaths? There was the supposed villa that M. Arnold was to be building for Mlle Violette. But had that been a front, a cover for something else? If Mlle Violette had not in fact been M. Arnold's latest client, then what had she been?

And then there was the hotel safe break-in. I cast my mind to the night in Monte Carlo, which now seemed so long ago. M. Arnold had made a comment about the antiquity of the safe at the hotel. Was knowledge about safes a skill architects usually had?

Hotel gossip still had not elucidated the exact nature of the letter taken from the safe. Was it a love letter, as initially suspected, or was it a document related to the war as I now conjectured? Had M. Arnold known something about the theft?

Could Baron Tacotti have been talking to M. Arnold yesterday in the garden? Had the Baron's warning been a threat?

Thinking about the Baron, I looked around the breakfast room. "Has anyone seen Baron Tacotti this morning?"

My breakfast companions looked around the room as well and shook their heads.

Just then, the doors of the salon crashed open, and in walked the Commissary Juneau of the police. He paused at the double door, legs opened, hands on hips, a perfect replica of Russian proletariat propaganda posters. All he was missing was a red flag flapping behind him.

He scanned the room, and his gaze paused when he met mine. He lingered on my face, but I didn't cower. Presently, he moved on. I noticed the moment he spied his prey and followed his line of sight.

"Mlle Rosalie," he said for the entire room to hear. At that moment, even those guests who hadn't interrupted their breakfast upon his entrance laid down their tea spoons and turned to follow his progress across the room to Mlle Rosalie's table.

I turned back to the door. In the vacated door frame stood M. Francois, doing his nervous side step shuffle. I liked M. Francois, but I wished he would stand up to that bully.

"Mlle Rosalie," the Commissary said, and I turned my attention back to him. Having reached Mlle Rosalie's table, he seized her by the arm and said, "Will you please escort me to the police station?"

Mlle Rosalie became flustered. "I don't understand," she protested, and she attempted to gather her gloves and bag from the table with one hand. She looked around the room, helpless. "I don't understand," she repeated. "What is this about?"

"We have some questions in connection with M. Arnold's death," the Commissary said curtly, and led her stiffly by the arm.

As the Commissary and Mlle Rosalie made their way out of the breakfast room, guests averted their eyes as she passed.

I really disliked that man. Was it really necessary to cause such a scene? To humiliate Mlle Rosalie in such a manner? A woman, whose social standing had already tumbled quite considerably since being rejected by Lord Withermorlington in favor of Mlle Violette and then deserted by M. Arnold before her villa...Oh, perhaps, on second thought, the Commissary knew what he was doing after all. But I still did not approve of his methods.

"How exciting," gushed Lady Morton. "To think, a real killer was hiding in our midst."

I raised a quizzical eyebrow.

"Oh, my dear," said Lady Morton in response. "I never really suspected you." She placed a gloved hand on top of mine. "I knew the police had to be wrong about you. Not when you are of such impeccable pedigree. Now, chorus girls, they are quite different…"

I quite preferred it when Lady Morton had been avoiding me.

"Lady Morton," I said, "in the case of M. Arnold, we don't know if there has been a murder."

"Oh, you mark my words, when you've seen as much of life as I have…I'm quite positive it's murder."

CHAPTER 24

It turned out that Lady Morton had been quite right in being quite positive. M. Arnold's death looked like murder.

The news circulated the hotel soon after breakfast. I really couldn't understand how the news made its way so quickly from the police station to the hotel. I said as much as I was acquainting Uncle Albert with the latest developments while going through his correspondence.

Wilford cleared his throat discreetly. "If I may throw some light on the problem, My Lady?"

"Yes, Wilford, that would be most kind."

"The boy who delivers vegetables to the kitchen is the son of the second cousin of the wife of the local police sergeant's brother-in-law." Wilford must have seen the confusion in my face, because he clarified. "Or put another way, the wife of the local police sergeant is the sister-in-law of the second cousin—"

"You're saying the kitchen staff has access to

information straight from the police station?" I interrupted Wilford before things got even more complicated.

"It would appear so."

"So, what is the latest news?" I asked.

"While I was down in the kitchens preparing your uncle's mid-morning glass of warm milk,"—I shuddered slightly. I couldn't imagine anyone who had graduated from the nursery room for good wanting such a beverage—"the staff were having an impromptu mid-morning assembly. I happened to overhear that the case against Mlle Rosalie is quite damning. She was not only seen arguing with M. Arnold by the cliff at the base of which he was later discovered, but it now appears that she owed M. Arnold a substantial sum of money. No doubt Lord Withermorlington's unfortunate transfer of affections to a new lady friend, namely Mlle Violette, caused a considerable impediment in Mlle Rosalie's flow of funds. Mlle Rosalie, however, insists that the money was due to M. Arnold only upon completion of her villa. Since the villa had not been completed to the exacting stipulations of their building contract, Mlle Rosalie refused to make a payment."

"A sound business decision," my uncle inserted.

"But unfortunately, it makes her a suspect," I added. "What about the murder of Mlle Violette and the stolen letter? What does the kitchen staff say about that?"

"The theories on those two counts," Wilford answered, "run along the lines already established by the hotel's guests." Wilford had such a dignified way of labeling gossip. "The chief reason for Mlle Violette's murder was that she had usurped Mlle Rosalie's place on the social ladder. Mlle Violette did not have the decency to wait for Mlle Rosalie's villa to be complete and for the grand parties envisioned by Mlle Rosalie to commence before becoming Lord Withermorlington's mistress.

"Mlle Violette even had the impertinence of threatening to build a villa quite near Mlle Rosalie. But perhaps that was due to the fact that both women were building on land awarded to them by Lord Withermorlington, rather than due to any true malice on Mlle Violette's part. Though I now understand that a villa might not have been entirely in the stars for Mlle Violette. Nevertheless, the kitchen staff agree that these are most grievous transgressions that Mlle Rosalie could not rightly overlook."

"Does the kitchen staff have any other theories about Mlle Violette's death?" I wanted to see if any of them had gotten wind of her double agent role during the war.

"Not to my knowledge."

"And what do the oracles of the kitchens make of the safe break-in and the missing letter?"

"The exact nature of the letter removed from the safe remains a mystery, even for the kitchen staff. The letter has not been located, and neither has the culprit. But as I understand, Baron Tacotti has disappeared. Most telling, don't you think, My Lady?"

Ah! So he had indeed disappeared. "I quite agree," I said. "I also believe that Baron Tacotti's disappearance is not coincidental." Whether it was an admission of guilt, I could not say.

The Baron had admitted in the garden his involvement in the safe break-in, but seemed to stop short of admitting murdering Mlle Violette. I wondered whether his companion in the garden had been M. Arnold, and whether the Baron had pushed M. Arnold off the cliff and subsequently disappeared. But that couldn't be because M. Arnold was supposed to have been by Poppy's side yesterday afternoon, looking at villas, so he could not have been in the garden. And what about the Baron's reference to Bad Ragaz, the spa town in Switzerland? Had M. Arnold ever been to Switzerland?

"Damn funny business," Uncle Albert piped up, but that was the extent of his contribution to the conversation, and he returned to the botanical volume in his lap. As the murder affair concerned plants only marginally—in the form of the belladonna poison used on Mlle Violette—the case failed to hold my uncle's interest.

The exchange of news concluded as Wilford excused himself to go press some trousers, and I returned to my uncle's correspondence.

I continued to turn over the facts in my head. It seemed so far no one suspected Mlle Violette of being anything more than a chorus girl and a mistress to a string of well-connected men. But what if the crime for which she was punished happened before her time with Lord Withermorlington? I needed to find more about Mlle Violette and M. Arnold, but I wasn't sure how.

CHAPTER 25

My break came the next morning, from the most unlikely place. While a prodigious number of hotel guests had left for Mlle Violette's funeral, I declined to attend. I did not know the woman, and given her background, my attendance did not seem appropriate.

Uncle Albert was engrossed in whatever the Royal Society for Natural History Appreciation's members did all day. Mostly, they gathered in the Petit Salon just off the atrium, smoking cigars, reading the daily press, and exchanging clever tidbits about flowers and such things, I presumed. They left the salon only at mealtimes, stretched their legs—as far as their various individual ailments allowed—on the promenade at dusk, and then returned to the salon in the evening for drinks, billiards—for those whose rheumatism didn't impede the game—and some bridge.

Bridge games, however, were the domain of the matrons of the hotel, who gathered in the Grand Salon each evening—under its famous stained glass dome, designed by Gustave Eiffel himself, and a Baccarat crystal chandelier—to play late into the night. The salon, adjacent to the hotel lobby, and separated only by a series of colonnades, had the added advantage of giving the matrons a convenient view of the hotel's entrance and thus an uninterrupted view of the comings and goings of the other hotel guests.

As Poppy was keeping to her room this morning, I idled about the hotel. I lingered on the terrace after breakfast, walked the atrium and the Grand Salon, empty now as its habitual occupants were at the funeral, and eventually made my way to the gardens. There I idled some more and walked down the terraces to look at the avenue of Greek statues.

Sitting on a marble bench between the statues of Athena and Themis, I saw the most unlikely figure. The elaborate hat, slightly unsuitable for the time of day and occasion, was unmistakable. It was Mlle Rosalie. But what was she doing here?

Curiosity eclipsed decorum in that moment, and I approached her, even though we hadn't been formally introduced.

"Mlle Rosalie," I addressed her, "may I join you?" I motioned to the empty half of the bench.

She removed the ivory cigarette holder from her mouth, exhaled, while looking at me from under the brim of her hat, and nodded.

"I'm Lady Caroline," I said, unsure how to initiate the conversation I was hoping we'd have.

I had formed an idea that Mlle Rosalie might be in a position to give me more information about Mlle Violette and M. Arnold. After all, she had been acquainted with both.

"*Oui*, I know who you are," she said, which surprised me. I took a seat beside her. She unfastened the large jewel clasp on a gold cigarette case, as ostentatious as her hat, and offered me a cigarette.

"No, thank you."

"You are not at the funeral?" she said.

I shook my head. "I didn't really know Mlle Violette."

"Has not stopped most other people," she said. "What a spectacle it must be."

I didn't reply. I could not imagine what a funeral of a notorious mistress, attended by her lover and his new mistress, and scores of people who were there only out of curiosity rather than genuine grief was like. The only funeral I had attended had been for my brother.

We stood in silence for a few moments, each lost in her own thoughts.

But though memories of my brother flooded in, I was on a mission. Providence had given me a chance to learn more about the victims, and I wasn't about to waste it. Sitting under the gaze of Athena, I hoped the goddess of wisdom would guide me in my impromptu interview.

"I'm glad to see the matter with the police has

been resolved in your favor," I said.

She exhaled a long and elegant puff of smoke. "Yes, I still have a few friends left in high places. A certain admirer at the Ministry of Justice, in Paris, secured my release."

"Are the police going to pursue the case against you?"

"They don't have much. Just some inconclusive speculations." I turned to watch her as she spoke. Though my initial impression of her had been of a pretty and naive ornamental doll, I now saw that she was more shrewd and self-assured than I had supposed. She spoke with a calmness and confidence that belied her decorative appearance.

I wondered how to introduce Mlle Violette or M. Arnold into the conversation. I could have pursued her mention of the funeral, but it felt wrong. M. Arnold, I decided, presented a safer topic. "What will you do now about the villa? I asked. "I mean, with M. Arnold…" I hoped she would pick up the thread.

"You mean, with M. Arnold dead?" she said.

I nodded.

"I'm not sure. These recent events have been a bit much for me. I pictured my years after the 'Folies Bergere' club in Paris as pleasant and quiet. I'd had enough drama and intrigue while dancing. Perhaps I'll go back to Paris. Or I'll travel Europe again. Perhaps I will go to England for a while," she said and looked at me.

"Was life at the Folies very competitive? Were the dancers in competition for gentlemen?"

"Oh, yes. Only the prettiest girls and the best dancers make it into the troupe. And a girl's time in the troupe is short-lived. The strain on the body, you see. The dance numbers are quite demanding on the body. Have you ever seen one of our shows?"

I shook my head and could feel my cheeks burning intensely.

"Don't be so scandalized," Mlle Rosalie replied. "Many gentlemen bring their mistresses to see the shows. It's quite respectable in Paris." She took a drag from her cigarette holder and exhaled before continuing. "Anyhow, a dancer has a short time to make the most of it, to secure her old age—gifts of money, jewels, a house, if she's lucky—before her body is broken, and the long hours, the smoking, the drinking, and the late nights ruin her beauty. A girl has to be smart about her choices, otherwise she will end up an old hag, selling flowers on the street…" She drifted off, as though thinking of her impending old age. I wondered if she knew many such women.

"May I ask you about Mlle Violette?" I asked, and threw her a furtive glance.

Mlle Rosalie stared at the distance, her eyes tensed into slits, and took the time to inhale from her cigarette holder and exhale before answering. "Very well," she said. "What would you like to know?"

"Were you two friends, before, at the Folies?" I said.

She shook her head. "When I came to Paris, I was naive. A pretty girl from the provinces, looking to become an actress or to dance. I was naive, but not desperate. It took me a while to move up in the ranks of the chorus and learn my way around men. But I did." She looked at me with no timidity in her eyes. "I came to realize," she continued, "that my most useful tool was my outward naivete. I cultivated it to perfection and used it to manipulate men to get what I wanted. Nothing gets a man as excited as an inexperienced damsel in distress."

While she took another pull from her cigarette, I wondered why she was being so candid with me. Perhaps, as I was neither a man to charm, nor a woman with whom to compete for a man's attention, she didn't need to pretend. Perhaps she had no genuine friends to confide in…

"And then Violette came along." Her tone darkened. "She had grown up on the streets of Paris. Not homeless, but with an unpleasant upbringing. Her parents ran a bar in a Parisian slum. Violette had risen through the criminal underbelly of Paris, as the mistress of one gangster or another. By the time she arrived at the Folies, at 18, she was done with the uncouth life of the criminal classes and had set her sights on the pampered life of the aristocracy. And she was ruthless. She would stop at nothing to get what she wanted. Unfortunately for me, what she wanted was what I had. She saw me at the height of my career, the mistress of aristocrats, spoiled with jewels, clothes, and gallant attention. So she set out to get what I had. Through some talent and a lot of bullying, she became the star of the show. She snatched Lord Withermorlington, who was the most generous of the patrons, away from me, and was about to build a bigger and better villa than mine."

"Is that how she met M. Arnold? Through the villa?" I asked, although I suspected the connection between them was not a villa.

"Oh, no," Mlle Rosalie said and laughed, her voice ringing like a crystal bell across the garden. "M. Arnold, Gilles Arnold, was always hanging about at the Folies Bergere. He was fascinated by Violette, drawn by her animalistic instinct for survival. They were probably kindred spirits—two urchins looking to make it big."

"What was M. Arnold's background?" I asked, intrigued by Mlle Rosalie's description of him.

"M. Arnold began coming to the Folies when he was a student at L'Ecole des Beaux-Arts, studying architecture. He was from Belgium, I believe. He supported himself by installing safes throughout Paris; his father had been a locksmith. The girls in the troupe knew when M. Arnold had installed a safe for a rich client, because he was uncommonly generous with his tips that night."

Mlle Rosalie's mention of safes reminded me of M. Arnold's comment about the hotel's safe. My mind raced. I had overheard Baron Tacotti confess he broke into the safe, but what if I had heard wrong? What if M. Arnold had broken into the safe instead? It was worth exploring.

"When did M. Arnold come to the Riviera?" I said.

"Let me think, it must have been around 1922."

"I noticed he was a gambler. He lost lots of money the other night in the casino."

Mlle Rosalie turned her gaze to me. I could see that behind her eyes she was speculating about the nature of my questions, but answered, "Yes. But he always seemed to find more."

As Mlle Rosalie had been candid with me, I made up my mind to be blunt. "Do you think it was M. Arnold who broke into the hotel's safe?"

She laughed. "Why would he do that?"

"I don't know," I said. I didn't wish to tell her that I thought Mlle Violette and M. Arnold were planning a blackmail scheme, or that Mlle Violette had been a spy, or that I suspected M. Arnold had a history of breaking into safes, that his celebrations in Paris happened after bountiful hauls.

We sat in silence for a few moments. Since Mlle Rosalie was quite familiar with Mlle Violette and M. Arnold, I wondered if she might know what had been hidden in the safe. "Do you have any inkling of what might have been taken?" I said.

"None at all," she replied. "It's the strangest thing, no? Why would the thief not take the jewels?" She laughed at the absurdity of it.

Why indeed.

I wanted to ask if she knew who had killed Mlle Violette and M. Arnold, assuming his death was indeed a murder and not just an accident, but decided against it. Even if she knew, or had her suspicions, she probably would not share it with me. Such unguarded confidences might expose both of us to harm.

Instead, we spoke about the Riviera season and the upcoming exhibition match of Suzanne Lenglen. The celebrated French tennis player was coming to Cannes, and the hotel was abuzz with excitement at seeing this Olympic, French Open, and Wimbledon champion play. I had seen her at Wimbledon in 1922, where she won the title in a game lasting only 26 minutes. Her style of play was as legendary as her titles, leaping across the court in aerial jumps in a manner that rivaled M. Francois.

After a while, Mlle Rosalie excused herself, as she had a lunch appointment with a potential benefactor for the villa fund.

I thanked Mlle Rosalie for her time and sat under the statue of Athena, thinking.

What if M. Arnold was the hotel thief and someone killed him for what he took from the safe? I suspected he was behind the spate of safe break-ins across the Riviera. I also had no doubt now that he had been Mlle Violette's accomplice during the war. Had they discovered something important? Something important enough that got them both killed? But what?

CHAPTER 26

Although engrossed in the mystery of Mlle Violette's and M. Arnold's deaths, I did not fail to notice that Poppy had begun quoting Keats with increasing regularity at teatime and dinner. It was clear to me that she was pining after the loss of not one, but two objects of affection—M. Arnold and the missing Baron Tacotti.

Thus, I decided it was time to take Poppy's mind off her lost lovers, and in the process perhaps even come across some other unworthy men for her to fixate on.

With the help of the hotel concierge, I devised a smashing plan.

Soon after breakfast the next morning, Poppy and I set off for Hotel du Cap in Antibes. The crowning glory of the hotel was Eden Roc —a beach complex of white rock terraces at one end of the property cascading down to the Mediterranean. Just a few years before the war, the owners had blasted a seawater swimming pool right into the cliff. It was heaven. The adjacent Sea Pavilion, which served a decent lunch on a grand terrace overlooking the azure water, was not bad either.

A morning of lounging by the pool and sunbathing was followed by a quick lunch on the said terrace of the Pavilion. Relaxing, with the refreshing breeze in my hair, I wished we were staying at Hotel du Cap rather than in Nice. But I could tell that the bohemian atmosphere of the place and its youthful energy—made even more fashionable by the Murphys' stay at the hotel a few years ago—would not appeal to the members of the Royal Society.

After lunch, we drove towards Grasse, the perfume capital of the world, away from the sea towards the hills and mountains encircling the coast. We left the bustle of the resorts behind, and the scenery changed to a tranquil countryside dotted with ancient villages—clusters of stone houses clinging to hill tops.

Dominated by grand perfume factories and surrounded by fields that grew the flowers whose essence was used in perfumes across the world, enchanting fragrance permeated the narrow streets of Grasse.

My plan for Grasse was to distract Poppy with visits to perfume factories, perfume shops, and perhaps even to stop at Count Karowsky's greenhouses and fields just outside town. With any luck, the Count might even be there to give us a tour.

After a visit to the gardens of the Maison Molinard, where we learned about extracting oils and essence, we headed to Perfumerie Toussaint, a purveyor of the finest scents, recommended to me by the hotel's concierge.

The grandson of the founder of the perfumery, the current M. Toussaint, proved to be welcoming and affable. As we tried scent after scent, I could see Poppy's mood finally lifting. M. Toussaint walked us through top notes, the heart of fragrances, and base notes. It all sounded more complicated than an opera score.

We were thus completing the purchase of a few bottles when I glanced at the display of men's scents. There, a fanciful bottle of cologne caught my attention. Rectangular, made of red glass with a gold metal lattice overlay, it bore, in intricate gold letters, a name I recognized—Bodin.

I gazed at the name for a while, trying to place it. And finally, I realized it was one of the names on the list Jane had sent me of Mlle Violette's known lovers.

As M. Toussaint had been so forthcoming, I resolved to ask him a few questions about the name.

"M. Toussaint," I began, "that is a beautiful bottle," pointing to the ornate, old-fashioned design.

"*Oui*, Mademoiselle, very well spotted. That is one of the masterpieces of the late M. Bodin," he began.

"Late?" I asked.

"*Oui*, he died just last year. In the prime of his career. Of course, as you may know, he was one of Tsar Nicolas' premier perfumers, but alas, the Revolution drove him to Paris. But with a talent like his, he could work anywhere. He quickly made a name for himself among the great perfumers of France."

He took a bottle off the glass shelf and uncapped it. I smelled the scent and tried not to pull an offensive face. The smell was heavy and cloying. Reminiscent of billy goats running recklessly through a field of ripe freesias, I wondered how anyone could find the fragrance attractive. But then again, the singular smell probably appealed to a man like the Tsar, notorious for his penchant for Faberge eggs.

I smiled at M. Toussaint and tried to hold my breath until such time as he removed the bottle from under my nose.

In the meantime, Poppy was surveying the glass shelves of men's scents, no doubt mentally selecting a gift for one of the dashing American gentlemen we had met at Eden Roc. She had arranged dinner with one of them for this evening.

Something in my mind stirred, and I knew I needed to know more about M. Bodin.

"A truly magnificent scent," I said, looking for a way to guide the conversation in the direction

I wanted it to go. Poppy, who had just smelled the bottle, threw me a quizzical look, but did not contradict me. "Such a loss for the perfume world. Do you know how he died?"

"Oh, yes. Most tragic. There was a break-in at his Place Vendome apartment in Paris. I'm not sure what was taken, but he suffered a heart attack as a result. Sadly, I could not attend his funeral."

So there had been another robbery. What did these robberies have in common? Were they all perpetrated by the same person? Or were they all in search of the same thing?

"His death came at an inopportune time," the perfumer continued. "I believe he was working on a new formula. He had made an appointment to come down to Grasse, but his death prevented it."

"You think he was working on a new perfume?" I said.

"I could not be sure. Of course, he could have been coming down to Grasse for a different reason, but he was interested in visiting the different flower growers in the area. Perfumers usually do that when they have a certain smell in mind. Alas, no new formula was discovered in his notes, so perhaps his planned trip was for another purpose altogether."

"A formula?"

He nodded. "*Oui*, any perfumer would record his formulas and experiments, much like a chef or a chemist," he said.

I nodded back in return. M. Toussaint had been most helpful. And after finding a delicate way to refuse his offer of purchasing a bottle of the exquisite perfume de Bodin, we departed.

"What were you playing at, Gassy?" Poppy asked as we made our way to our red two-seater parked in the town square.

"Nothing," I lied. I wasn't sure whether to take Poppy into my confidence. She lacked tact sometimes, especially when in the company of handsome men. And I myself was not sure what exactly I had stumbled upon. I suspected it was all related and important, but I needed time to work it out in my mind.

I was glad that when we stopped by Count Karowsky's greenhouses, we were informed that he was, unfortunately, out. The gardens were beautiful, with flowers in early bloom. A rambling stone villa, typical for Provence, with a red-tiled roof and blue shutters, unfurled across one end of the vast property.

But I was no longer in the mood for flowers. The pieces of information from the perfumer, M. Toussaint, and from Mlle Rosalie, were vying for attention. And I needed to take time and make sense of them. I was sure they came together to make a story, but I wasn't sure what that story was.

I feared Count Karowsky's absence would be a blow to Poppy's lifting mood, but as she switched to quoting Wordsworth on our drive back to the hotel, admiring the sublime beauty of the landscape, I knew the worst had passed.

As we drove back to Nice, Poppy at the wheel, my mind raced over the facts in sync with the countryside rushing by me. Poppy took advantage of the time to Nice to enumerate the merits of each of the frocks she had just received from Paris, and wondered which one to wear to dinner this evening. I took advantage of her monologue to piece together all I knew of Mlle Violette and M. Arnold and the hotel robbery.

The son of a locksmith, M. Arnold had worked as a safe installer in Paris during his studies. He'd spent money freely after installing safes. I wondered now if Mlle Rosalie's reference to his spending habits was a covert way of alluding to her suspicion that M. Arnold had been a thief. Perhaps.

Mlle Rosalie had also made clear that there was an evident attraction between Mlle Violette and M. Arnold. Whether that attraction resolved itself into an affair or a working relationship, I was not sure. But as Mlle Violette had been a double agent during the war, noted for her ability to obtain sensitive documents hidden in safes, I chose to assume that M. Arnold had been her accomplice.

In 1922, which was three years ago, M. Arnold had moved to the Riviera and became the architect of choice among the villa-building foreigners. Here was where the story became complicated. The series of safe break-ins that had happened on the Riviera, culminating with the break-in at the hotel, were only recent. If M. Arnold was behind them, why had he taken a pause between 1922 and now?

I moved to the information from the perfumer in Grasse. I knew from Jane that Mlle Violette had been M. Bodin's mistress. Given Mlle Violette's history, she was most likely the one behind the robbery at M. Bodin's apartment. M. Bodin had then died of a heart attack following the robbery. Presumably he died because something important was taken from him. He may have been working on a new perfume, but a formula was not found among his belongings. Had Mlle Violette stolen the perfume formula? And who had helped her break into the safe? M. Arnold had moved to the Riviera by then. But maybe he went back to Paris to assist her?

Was this formula the paper that was stolen from the hotel safe? Who took it? Baron Tacotti? M. Arnold? And where was the formula now?

And what about the rumor that Mlle Violette was going to establish a business on the Riviera? Perhaps I had been wrong that she was planning to blackmail old lovers. Perhaps she had been planning to produce a perfume.

But what about the fact that M. Bodin had worked for the Tsar in Russia? Was that important? Did that have anything to do with Mlle Violette's role as a double agent during the war? Instead of a perfume formula, were some important documents, pertaining to the war, taken from M. Bodin?

I needed a way to find more about the robberies, and I knew how. It was a long-shot, but it was a start.

Arriving back at the hotel in Nice, Poppy swanned off to get ready for the evening, having settled on a scarlet beaded frock, complemented by a mink stole and a sprinkling of rubies, and to no doubt bathe in her newly acquired scents, in the hope of fending off any competition in a four-mile radius. I proceeded to send a telegram to London.

This time, I wrote to Elanor—she who was placed by my mother at Lloyd's.

My telegram read: "Need info Bodin robbery in Paris '24. Lover Violette. M Arnold robber?"

I hoped the clues would be sufficient for Elanor to get some information. As the preeminent insurer of the rich and famous, Lloyd's would have information not only on its own policies, but would also have records of any major robberies and insurance payouts across the continents. Or at least, I reasoned, that would be the case. Given M. Bodin's address in Paris, I assumed, or rather hoped, his insurance policy, and accompanying payout, was worthy enough to catch Lloyd's attention.

At the same time, I also wondered if there was a war connection to M. Bodin's death, so decided it was prudent to send Jane at the War Office another telegram. "M Bodin spy?" it read.

My evening passed in nervous pacing across my suite. I considered joining the matrons in a game of Bridge, but came to my senses before walking into that particular trap.

CHAPTER 27

The first of the sun's rays next morning found me waiting in the Grand Salon. I had assumed this key position so that the messenger boys would have no trouble locating me when the telegram from London came through. But after a few hours, and more tea and pastries than was healthy, I went for a game of tennis.

Like everyone else, I was looking forward to Suzanne Lenglen's match tomorrow. Inspired by Mme Lenglen's upcoming visit, I wanted to practice some jumps I had picked up watching her.

Plus, it was preferable to waiting around the salon. The location had two major flaws—it was open on all sides, and thus one could not avoid a stealthy attack by a matron appearing from behind a colonnade, and two, it was the favorite feeding ground of Lady Morton.

As I was chasing a few balls around the court, a messenger boy came running with a telegram. I motioned to my partner, a nice girl from London due to be presented at court next month, who had just arrived with her mother, that I needed a break and went to sit under a palm tree.

It was news from Lloyd's: "String robberies Paris '18-'22. Bodin papers jewels stolen. Died after robbery. Son filed claim from Switzerland. No record of Arnold. Safe breaks in Riviera from '25 same as Paris. Lloyd agent on Riviera. Jane says B not spy."

I read the telegram a few times. I wished Elanor had not been so frugal. For once, I appreciated my mother's loquacious communications. I was hoping a letter might be forthcoming on The Blue Train, but there was no indication in her communication of that. Perhaps I could telephone London later.

But I was sure I got the gist of Elanor's message: The safe break at M. Bodin's was part of a string of robberies in Paris between 1918 and 1922. Papers and jewels were taken from M. Bodin's apartment. M. Bodin's son had filed a claim, presumably with Lloyd's, from Switzerland for the stolen items. The same robberies were now happening on the Riviera, presumably by the same person or gang. Lloyd's had no record of M. Arnold. And there was a Lloyd's agent here on the Riviera. Plus, M. Bodin was not a war spy or agent.

Though short, the telegram was quite informative once deciphered. Two items caught my attention immediately—M. Bodin had a son, and Lloyd's had an agent on the Riviera.

As always, the communications from my

operatives in London raised as many questions as they cleared: Who was behind the string of robberies in Paris and on the Riviera? Presumably, the criminal had left Paris in 1922, when the robberies stopped, and was now operating on the Riviera. The dates coincided with M. Arnold's move to the Riviera in 1922. But why had no robberies occurred on the Riviera between 1922 and 1925?

I let my mind explore that particular question. M. Arnold had been an extremely successful architect, thus, I reasoned, he had not needed to resort to breaking into safes. But lately, as Mlle Rosalie had alluded, and as I had witnessed, he was losing more money than ever at the tables. Perhaps little gifts from lady friends were no longer enough to tie him over? Perhaps he felt the need to go back to his old ways? This would also explain why he might have traveled to Paris to assist Mlle Violette in the robbery of M. Bodin after such a long break.

Thinking of M. Bodin, I could no longer ignore the news that had captured my attention and my imagination the moment I had read it—M. Bodin had a son.

What had eluded me for so long now became clear. I had been troubled by the lack of a strong connection between the hotel robbery, Mlle Violette's murder, and M. Arnold's death. Mlle Rosalie's predicaments had explained only some of the clues. But a son, avenging his father's untimely death, was a powerful motive for murder.

I now arrived at the second curious piece of information—this son had filed a claim from Switzerland. I knew with certainty that Baron Tacotti had been in Switzerland. He had studied there and had mentioned a lawyer in Switzerland to his companion in the garden.

Hector, Lord Fetherly's secretary, had also spent time in Switzerland. On that count, Hector also qualified for the position of M. Bodin's son.

Perhaps so did many other men at the hotel, I told myself. As I had no idea how old M. Bodin had been when he died or how old his son was, I could not even begin to fathom who his son could be.

But I had to begin my search for M. Bodin's son somewhere, and all the clues pointed to Baron Tacotti—he admitted breaking into the hotel's safe, he had lived in Switzerland, and he had now disappeared. Plus, that old-fashioned mustache on one so young was suspicious.

I needed to check Baron Tacotti's true identity, and for that I needed to make an international telephone call.

CHAPTER 28

"Hello, Frau Baumgartnerhoff," I yelled down the telephone line in M. Francois' office. It had taken several exchanges to reach Frau Baumgartnerhoff in Switzerland and the connection was poor. "Can you hear me?"

"Yes, I hear you," she whispered back.

We yodeled back and forth a few more times, exchanging niceties and general enquiries after health and happiness, and I regretted not sending her a telegram instead.

"Frau Baumgartnerhoff, I have a small request," I said and gave her instructions on the information I required. I was not entirely certain she could acquire said information, but having spent character-building time with her, I knew she was a resourceful woman.

The call from Frau Baumgartnerhoff came back only a few hours later. I tried to ignore the look M. Francois gave me while I was closing the door to his office, with him on the outside, to take the call.

"I phoned the school," Frau Baumgartnerhoff

was saying. "Baron Tacotti is who he claims to be. He is not the son of M. Bodin." My heart sank. I had pinned all my hopes on Baron Tacotti. "But," came the faint voice of my former Finishing School Mistress over the line, "he paid the school fees for a student—" her voice cut out.

"Who paid fees for a student?"

"M. Bodin. For a student named Arkadii Go— unov." The connection crackled.

"What? I didn't get the name," I yelled. "It sounded like Gorunov."

"No, Godunov."

"Godunov. I got it," I yelled back. "Thank you!"

I placed the receiver down and leaned on M. Francois' desk. My mind rejoiced. M. Bodin's son was named Arkadii Godunov. But a fresh problem crystallized—I had no idea who Arkadii Godunov was. All I had to go on was that the name sounded Russian and that he had been at school with Baron Tacotti. And since Baron Tacotti was missing, I could not rely on him to reveal Arkadii Godunov's true identity.

About to leave M. Francois' office, a thought stopped me in my tracks. Was it not conceivable that the person Baron Tacotti was talking to in the garden had been this Godunov?

As far as I could make it out, Mr. Godunov had asked Baron Tacotti to break into the hotel safe and steal something Mlle Violette had deposited in it; the something being a paper she had stolen in Paris, with the help of M. Arnold, from M. Bodin, his father. Baron Tacotti had agreed because Mr. Godunov had helped the Baron in Bad Ragaz. Then Mr. Godunov had killed Mlle Violette, and then M. Arnold, as revenge for his father's death. Baron Tacotti had objected to the murders and had vanished.

So far, so good. Now all I had to do was find Mr. Godunov.

As I headed for the door, I noticed it was ajar. I wondered how many people had heard my telephone conversation. But as I exited the manager's office, the only person standing around, and showing any interest in me, was the manager himself.

"Thank you, M. Francois," I said and smiled sweetly, hoping my smile would compensate for the inconvenience I had caused him.

M. Francois bowed slightly, but perhaps with less than his usual grace.

On second thought, I decided to add a few extra notes to his gratuity upon leaving.

An uncharitable thought, however, was forming in my mind as I watched M. Francois close the door of his office. Could M. Francois be M. Bodin's missing son? What did I really know about the manager? My family had been coming to the Hotel Paradis since I was a child, but M. Francois had become manager only after the war.

Where had he been before that? At the front? In

Switzerland, perhaps? He'd had ample opportunity to break into the hotel safe, or have Baron Tacotti do it for him, without fear of being discovered. He had also been there the night Mlle Violette came back from the casino. He hadn't been at the casino, but he had walked her up to her room. Could he have given Mlle Violette the fatal dose of poison at that time?

"Excuse me, Madam," a young bellboy pushing a cart stacked with luggage passed by me and drew me out of my thoughts. I shook my head. It was impossible. M. Francois was such a nice man.

I glanced at the clock in the lobby and realized that I hadn't been to my uncle's suite today. So much for being a good secretary.

"Young Carol," he said cheerfully as I walked in. "How is the hunt going?"

"Well enough," I said noncommittally. But the truth was, I had devoted no time to the flower in the past few days. "Oh, I'm sorry uncle, but I've just been so busy following clues concerning Mlle Violette's and Mr. Arnold's deaths."

"Who?" my uncle said.

"You know, the two people who died recently," I began.

"Nothing to do with us," he said. "Now, about The Golden Platypus, what are your plans for today?"

CHAPTER 29

I thus found myself, riddled with guilt for ignoring familial duties, walking the cliffs of Cote d'Azur. Disheartened by my lack of progress, my uncle had directed me to spend the rest of the afternoon seeking the mythical orchid on south-facing craigs. It was thanks to these instructions that a casual observer could see me now and again leaning uncertainly over bluff edges.

Here, away from the promenade and hotels, the coast was wild and untamed. The turquoise blue water lapped at the cliffs and I watched the birds, nesting along the bluffs, swoop through the air.

I only heard the steps behind me at the last moment, and by then it was too late to react. A hand shoved me hard, and I tumbled forward. Frantically I tried to grab onto some grass as I pitched over the edge, but it just slipped between my fingers. I screamed and closed my eyes for the descent. Though the water was beautiful, I preferred not to see it when my body collided with it. The last blade of grass cut through my skin and I plunged into free fall.

I met my end sooner than I had expected.

My feet hit solid ground, and I stopped falling. I opened my eyes and noted that I had landed on a small grassy outcrop not far from the edge above me. I gave a silent thanks to Frau Baumgartnerhoff, for it was the hiking boots, which she had ordered for each of her girls from an old shoemaker in the village of Zermatt, that had done the trick. The special spikes on the bottom of the boots were now gripping that grassy knoll for dear life.

I leaned back and glued my back against the vertical wall of the cliff. My heart thundered as loud as the waves below. I tried to slow down my breath and think of what to do next. Half-expecting to see my assailant lean over the edge to check if I had made contact with the rocks below, I wondered what he, or perhaps she, would do when he saw me perched here on the outcrop.

As I looked up, a head popped over the edge. My heart jumped. I held my breath.

"*Elle va bien!*" the head yelled. I got the impression that he was talking to someone behind him.

For a moment, I was disoriented. Was this my attacker? Or was this my attacker's accomplice telling him I was alive, and to come finish the job properly? I had never seen him in my life. He was wearing a peaked hat and I could discern a row of gold buttons.

"*Attends ici! Je reviens tout de suite!*" he yelled down to me. Actually, I thought to myself, I would prefer it if he didn't return. "*Un baton*, a stick, I will bring a stick!" he said to me in halting English and disappeared from view. I was rather hoping he wouldn't find a stick long enough to dislodge me from my grassy perch. But, undoubtedly, it was what he had to do. Resigned to my fate, now I just had to wait until he came back with a thick branch and pushed me off into the abyss.

But then, the most unexpected thing happened. The voice of Lady Morton sailed over the edge and crashed in waves over me. "What! Where is she? Lead me to her!"

Momentarily, Lady Morton's large hat, and then her face appeared over the edge. The peaked cap joined her. I was happy to see he was not brandishing a stick, yet.

"Lady Caroline!" Lady Morton exclaimed. "What are you doing down there, my dear?" she yelled down at me, exasperated.

"I was pushed, Lady Morton," I answered back, trying to keep my voice even as though not to betray my frustration at her question. It was not as though I had climbed down here out of my own volition. Though, given my uncle's varied and singular interests, an impartial observer might conclude that I was down here collecting specimens under his direction.

"Oh, you young people and your games!" she

reproached. "If you break something, what will your mother think of me? You have to be more careful, Lady Caroline. A young lady cannot run around cliffs like a goat." She paused to let the reprimand sink in. "I shall write to your mother presently," she threatened, "and inform her that this buffoonery has to stop."

"*Un peu d'aide?*" I pleaded for a bit of help with the man in the cap, who I now saw must be Lady Morton's chauffeur.

He nodded and disappeared. He presently reappeared and lowered a rope to me. I gave another silent thanks to Frau Baumgartnerhoff. It was owing to her, and her instructions on mountaineering, that I was now able to scale the side of the cliff. Digging the spikes of my hiking boots into the crumbly rock side, I moved slowly up. Three points attached at all times, moving only one hand or foot at a time.

And then I froze.

"*Arret!*" I yelled at the chauffeur, but he must not have heard my plea to stop, because he continued to pull with all his might. "Wait, please!" I called out to him.

What had halted me in my tracks was not fear, but a flat-winged bumblebee. I was sure of it. And right there, next to it, just within arm's reach, was the orchid. Or at least I thought it was. For now, it was just a green shoot with some green buds, but in a few days it would open up to be a beautiful milky orchid.

Just then, the chalky rock behind my feet crumbled, and I slipped down. I yelled and the brave chauffeur began pulling me back up. At last, my fingers were at the lip of the cliff and the chauffeur grabbed me by the hand and heaved the rest of my body over the edge. I lay there, hugging the grass, breathing in its scent, and the scent of life.

"Thank you!" I managed to breathe out as I lifted my head. I even managed to smile at the chauffeur. It was only then that I noticed that Lady Morton had not stopped talking, and had by now moved on to selecting which church in London would have the privilege to bless my union to Cecil.

I decided the monologue did not require a response and returned my thoughts to the green shoot on the cliff face. How was I ever going to get to the milky orchid once it bloomed? Perhaps Poppy would be willing to lend me a hand.

Now that I was sure I would live, my thoughts returned to the other important development of the last few minutes—whose was the hand that had pushed me over?

I got to my feet and brushed the dirt off my front as best as I could, then swept my hair out of my face.

"Lady Morton, Monsieur," I said with as much dignity as my grass stained dress would allow, "thank you for coming to my rescue. I am in your debt." But not enough to marry Cecil, I wanted to add, but bit my tongue. The chauffeur beamed at me and Lady Morton scowled. I wondered if she still thought I had done this on purpose to jeopardize her relationship with my mother.

"Did any of you see what happened? Did you see who pushed me over?" I asked.

"Pushed you over?" Lady Morton asked in surprise. "No one pushed you over, my dear."

I looked in confusion from her to her driver. "But I clearly felt someone push me. Did you not see who?" I protested.

"All we saw, coming round the bend, was you, falling forward over the cliff."

The woman was clearly unstable. I turned with pleading in my eyes to the chauffeur.

"It is true, Madame," he said. "From the road, driving up, we could only see the cliff face. We saw a body going over—yours. We couldn't see if there was someone behind you. By the time we drove to your spot, there was no one here."

"Are you sure you didn't just slip?" Lady Morton added.

I shook my head in disbelief, but didn't press the point.

"Now, my dear," Lady Morton said, grabbing me by the elbow. "Let me take you back to your uncle. He will know what to do with you." I wanted to protest. I was not a naughty child who had broken a window. But I was emotionally and physically exhausted all of a sudden, and I didn't have it in me to resist Lady Morton.

I indicated to the chauffeur to pick up my bicycle. And as I took my seat next to Lady Morton in the back of the car, the chauffeur tied the frame to the car's luggage rack, and drove off in the direction of the hotel.

I allowed Lady Morton to drone on about Cecil, and duty, and decorum without interrupting or contradicting her.

But I wasn't listening.

Instead, I reviewed all I knew about the case. I was sure M. Bodin's son had tried to kill me. And, if he'd felt threatened enough to push me off a cliff, it meant I was close to discovering the truth.

My assailant had seen me do or heard me say something that scared him. The problem was, I had no idea what that was. I was not nearer to knowing who the killer was than before I went over the cliff.

We drove back to the hotel and I let my gaze roam over the undulating countryside, its peaceful green fields soothing my troubled mind. And as we drove past a place I'd seen many times, I knew who was behind these crimes.

CHAPTER 30

"The closest one is here, in Nice," the concierge was saying.

"I'd rather not go to one in Nice," I said. "Is there another one?"

The concierge gave me a curious look, but proceeded, "There is a beautiful one in Menton."

"I'll go to Menton," I said.

"Tonight?" the concierge said. "It's over one hour's drive there. Another hour to get back. You will miss dinner."

I nodded. "Perhaps I'll go tomorrow morning," I said.

We had just arrived back at the hotel with Lady Morton and I had gone straight to the concierge's desk. I needed to rest. Perhaps the shock of being pushed off a cliff was catching up with me.

"Very well, I shall have the garage bring a car round for tomorrow after breakfast."

As I walked away, I remembered that Suzanne Lenglen's match in Cannes was tomorrow and if I went to Menton after breakfast, I'd miss it.

"Make it first thing in the morning," I told the concierge.

"Very well," he agreed, and made a note in his ledger.

My drive to Menton had given me the answer I was looking for, but the drive back had taken longer than expected.

A small rock slide had blocked off one lane on the Corniche Inferieure road. And with the French police trying to direct traffic consisting mostly of foreign tourists, confusion and misunderstanding had ensued.

I got back to the hotel perhaps too late to make it to the match in Cannes on time. I rushed to the concierge's desk. "How was your drive, Lady Caroline?" he asked.

"Satisfactory, thank you," I said. "Do you know if Lord Packenham's secretary, James, is still here? I'd like to leave a note for him. It's urgent."

By now, I had figured out that James was most likely Lloyd's agent on the Riviera. It explained his insistence to remain on the coast even after he was dismissed by my uncle, and more tellingly, he had been consulting with the police after the hotel break-in. I wanted to share with him what I had discovered. I wanted his advice on how to proceed.

"I'll try to deliver the note, but most guests have

already departed for Cannes."

I thanked him and made my way to my rooms. Just a few minutes later, a messenger boy arrived with a note from James, asking me to meet him in the hotel's garden.

I rushed down the grand staircase and through the French doors, out onto the verandah, and then down the stairs towards the lower garden terraces. I looked around, but couldn't see him, so I sat down on a bench to wait.

The perfume I had smelled on the day of my arrival preceded the soft footsteps. I tensed, but didn't turn around. I knew he had come.

He sat down, gently, on the bench beside me. "Hello, Lady Caroline."

"Hello, Count Karowsky," I said, trying to control my voice, but my trembling hands gave me away. "Or should I call you Arkadii Godunov?" I asked with more confidence than I felt.

"You may, if you wish," he said.

He leaned gently towards me and placed something cold against my spine. I shivered. I was sure it was a pistol.

Out of the pocket of his waistcoat, he extracted a small vial. "I'd like you to drink this," he said, his voice calm and cold.

"Why would I do that?" I said, barely able to whisper.

"To keep my secret. And because I have a gun to

your spine. If I pull the trigger, if the bullet doesn't kill you, it will for sure cripple you for life. The poison is cleaner and faster, trust me," he said.

He nudged the gun further into my spine. I took the bottle with a shaking hand. Traitorous hands, I chastised them. If I were going to die, I preferred my killer not to see my fear.

My mind reeled. I needed to buy myself time. Perhaps someone would come to my rescue. Why had I not confided in James earlier? Was there any hope that he would come to save me?

"If I am to die," I said, choosing to make my voice light and gracious, "be a gentleman and satisfy a few of my trifling curiosities."

"Of course, anything for a lady. But do not presume that anyone will come to rescue you. Everyone is at the tennis match. And the staff will not dare to intrude on a private, intimate meeting," he said.

"Are you not concerned that my death would raise questions?"

"What? The death of a suicidal young woman? I do not think so," he said, smiling a little.

"But I'm not suicidal," I pointed out.

"The police could be easily convinced that you are—throwing yourself off a cliff—"

"What? You pushed me!" I interrupted him.

"Ah! But Lady Morton is convinced that you jumped. I heard her tell the other women at dinner last evening how she had rescued you. It is not hard to conceive—the darling of the London scene, sent to work as a secretary for a batty old uncle. It's enough for anyone to wish to end their life."

He had a point, I conceded.

"I'm sure the police would think a third death suspicious," I continued to protest. I couldn't imagine that my death would go uninvestigated.

"You give the French police more credit than they are due. They are still trying to decide whether Mlle Violette's death was not actually a suicide—young women are so prone to them, you see—and whether M. Arnold did not slip to his death by accident. Yours would be just another one in a string of regrettable misfortunes."

"My informer from Switzerland would surely speak out when she hears of my death," I retorted, trying to convince the Count that his crimes would not go unpunished. I avoided mentioning Frau Baumgartnerhoff's name for her safety.

"I wouldn't worry about that. My connection with my Russian name has long been erased. You are one of only a few who know my true identity."

"What about Baron Tacotti?" I asked, remembering that they had been at school together and that he must surely know the Count's real name.

"He has his own reasons to hide the truth," the Count said simply.

"Bad Ragaz?" I asked, thinking back to the

conversation I had overheard in this same garden.

"Bad Ragaz," he confirmed.

Whatever had happened at Bad Ragaz had been grave enough to ensure the Baron's silence for life, I could see that clearly in the Count's nonchalant reaction.

I wondered, vaguely, if the Count had done away with the Baron as well, but decided that the precarious situation I currently found myself in was more pressing, and more deserving of my mental faculties.

I searched my brain for any other objection I could throw at Count Karowsky.

"And what if someone has seen you?" I asked in one final bid for my life.

"Most of the guests are by now at Mme Lenglen's match. Few would notice my absence when such talent is on display. And if a member of the hotel staff has seen my arrival," the Count continued, "I could claim that I was trying to talk you out of taking your life, but did not succeed." He shrugged almost apologetically.

As I sat in the garden, contemplating my last moments, my mind jumped inexplicably to my mother. I considered her telegram, and the fact that I could, at this moment, be sitting in a garden at Buckhill Place, the ancestral pile, on a stone bench much like this one, in the prettiest of gardens, secluded from the prying eyes of onlookers by blooming camellias, being wooed by

Leopold, whispering sweet nothings in my ear.

I considered my present situation a lucky escape.

The thought of my mother reminded me of another question I had for the Count. "Did you love your father?" I said.

"No, I absolutely abhorred him," he said with what I felt was cruel honesty.

I trembled lightly at his answer and the slight movement reminded me of the gun barrel resting against my spine.

The Count must have felt my shiver, because he continued, "He was a womanizing beast. While he paid for my education, he refused to send money and help to my mother once the revolution started in Russia. He left her there to die." His voice was hard.

"Then you didn't murder Mlle Violette in revenge for your father's death?" I asked.

"All I wanted from Mlle Violette was what was mine—the perfume formula. But she proved unreasonable and refused to give it to me. So she died."

"And Baron Tacotti got the formula for you out of the safe," I said.

He nodded.

"Is the Baron…unhurt?"

"He is quite well, sequestered somewhere in Italy. He decided it was not prudent to remain here. Perhaps understandably so."

"How did you know about the perfume? Had your father confided in you?" I asked, curiosity overtaking other instincts at the moment.

"I was the only person who knew about it. He wanted to use some of the more exotic flowers I was growing. He had developed the formula in his workshop and kept a small sample of it in his safe. I don't know how Mlle Violette found out about it. Maybe he showed it to her, the old fool." He paused for a moment. "It was to be his masterpiece, modern, fresh, like nothing else."

"And you smelled it on Mlle Violette that day in the lobby, when you led her away?" I said, thinking back to the morning of my arrival at Hotel Paradis. I'd heard Count Karowsky compliment Mlle Violette's perfume.

"I knew immediately she had been the one who'd broken into his safe. The smell was unmistakable. And she had come down here to the Riviera to try and sell the formula."

"Handing her a poisoned drink at the casino was easy enough," I said, my mind jumping to the night in Monte Carlo.

He nodded. "Inadvertently, Mlle Rosalie created the perfect distraction."

"And M. Arnold?"

"He had been her accomplice, of course. He confided in me one day, boasting about his escapades in Paris, and the break-ins here on the

Riviera. He was a scoundrel."

"And you just pushed him, like you pushed me?"

"Yes. Being business partners, no one would think anything of seeing us walk together along the bluffs. And poor Mlle Rosalie once again proved to be most useful. It was her argument with M. Arnold I had witnessed earlier that gave me the idea." He permitted himself an apologetic smile.

One last thing troubled my conscience. "You won't harm Poppy?" I turned to the Count.

He sneered. "Harm her? Why should I harm her?"

"She was in Grasse with me and heard my conversation with the perfumer. She could figure it all out."

He smiled, and his handsomeness struck me unexpectedly. Such a shame that he was a killer. "I doubt it," he said. "While I've been watching you, I've also formed the opinion that your friend's mind does not function in the same sophisticated manner as yours."

I blushed at the compliment. But flattery was futile. "And you will refrain from marrying her?" I said.

"Marry her?" he laughed, in a sincere manner without artifice. I presumed my impending fatal end created a bond of honesty between us. "Whatever gave you that idea?"

"Well, she's very well off. And she is enamored

with you. A lot of gentlemen would take advantage of such a situation," I explained my reasoning.

"I can set your mind at rest on that account," he said. "Your friend is quite safe with me. Her particular brand of well-fed Britishness does not appeal to me. You and I, though, could have made a great couple, and taken Britain and the Continent by storm."

I smiled demurely at this compliment as well. That he remained a gentleman even at such a difficult hour was to his credit.

"Just one last thing. How did you know I had figured it out?"

"I heard you on the phone, I heard you yelling my name down the line," he said and smirked.

"But how could you know I had linked the name to you?"

"Your trip to Menton. I heard you ask the concierge."

"But you could not have known I had you in mind," I protested.

"You would have pieced it all together soon enough. I decided to act before you had. And now, Lady Caroline," he pressed the pistol more forcefully into my back, "it's time. Don't make me use the gun. It's so unseemly and messy. It's an indignant way to go."

He leaned forward, and I felt his breath on my cheek. His movement was almost intimate, his face within kissing distance of my own. He took my hand in his and brought the little vial of poison up to my mouth. I drew my head back instinctively, but a renewed push of the unyielding metal against my spine brought my lips closer to the vial. He tipped the liquid towards my lips. For a moment, my mind traveled outside my body, and I mused that an onlooker would have assumed he was about to kiss me...

In the next moment, so many things occurred in succession that I was not sure exactly what happened.

A loud thud, as though a metal shovel striking a ripe pumpkin, and a gunshot.

I screamed and fell forward. My breath caught, and I had trouble breathing. I was waiting for the pain of my severed spine to reach my brain. But I could not feel anything. Perhaps my body was already paralyzed. My thoughts were confused. I wondered if I would die.

"That serves him right," came the booming voice of Poppy. Her shadow blocked out the light above me as she leaned over me. "Beastly," she exclaimed, "what are you doing rolling on the ground in such an unbecoming manner?"

She reached out a hand and pulled me up. I swayed, unsure if I could stand on my feet. After a moment's hesitation, my brain accepted that I was indeed able to balance on my own.

Still unclear about what had occurred, I shot a glance at Count Karowsky, collapsed as though sleeping on the soft grass, a folded garden chair discarded by his side.

"What happened?" I said, disoriented.

"Now, Gassy," Poppy said in a patronizing tone, "I do not hold you responsible. Men of such charm are difficult to resist. But I could not stand idly by when he tried to kiss you."

"But he didn't try to kiss me, he tried to kill me," I said, incredulous. How could Poppy have got it so wrong?

Poppy looked down at the heap, unconvinced.

"You could have killed him!" I said, pointing to the chair.

"Nonsense," Poppy replied, calm and collected. "I have long ago perfected my strike. I aim to mime, not kill. My backhand has always been particularly powerful."

I wasn't sure if she was referring to badminton or to hitting men over the head.

"But you could have killed me!" I cried, the foolishness of her actions just coming to me. "He had a gun against my back! He could have shot my spine out!"

Poppy blinked a few times. She leaned slightly backwards and looked at my back. "Oh, now that you mention it, the top button on the back of your dress appears to be missing. Shot clean, right off. Lucky break, eh, dodging the bullet like that?"

Perhaps, when Poppy hit the Count sideways,

the force of the impact made his hand slip, and as I fell forward, his bullet grazed my button, but I escaped with my life.

"Why are you not at the tennis match?" I said, the thought finally occurring to me.

"Well, I was on my way, I was running behind since I had changed my outfit a few times, the American dish was to be at the match, and as I was coming out of the lift, I saw you go toward the garden. I was about to call after you when I saw Count Karowsky follow you out. Curious as to what the two of you were up to, while the rest of us were at the tennis match, I followed him out. The bushes hid most of your bodies, but I could see that you were engaged in an intimate conversation. It was only when the Count leaned in to kiss you that I became enraged and grabbed the nearest chair to hit him."

"Why? Why hit him?" I said, unsure what had elicited such a reaction from Poppy.

"When he would join us during our villa outings with M. Arnold, he would be so gallant and forthcoming with his little compliments. I really thought his regard for me was growing. But at that moment, when I saw him kissing you, I realized he was an undeserving reprobate."

I stared at Poppy with incredulity, but was more than thankful for her rescue. "Thank you, Poppy," I said.

She linked her arm with mine, squeezed in a

vice grip, and led me up the steps of the garden.

CHAPTER 31

"And how did you come to realize that Count Karowsky was M. Bodin's son?" Lady Morton asked.

We were seated in the dining room of Hotel Paradis. After Count Karowsky's arrest, news of what had happened spread through the hotel, and somehow reached the tennis match in Cannes, so that as guests arrived back, they were fully aware of what had occurred in their absence.

Sensing this was a special occasion, M. Francois had reconfigured the dining room. All the individual tables were brought together in a row, and we were now sitting at a long banquet table. Pristine white tablecloths, exquisite china, crystal glasses, and silver candelabra lent the dinner a festive appearance.

A prevailing spirit of inquisitiveness had persuaded most of the hotel guests to join me for dinner—the Lords of the Royal Society and their secretaries, Lady Morton and the rest of the matrons, among many others. My uncle, through his association with me, was accorded the head of the table. I was sitting on his right.

At Lady Morton's question, the guests along the table leaned forward in unison, and directed their attention towards me.

"Well," I began, "it was only after hearing that M. Bodin was a Russian emigre and had a son that an event I had seen upon my arrival in Nice became clear. I had witnessed Baron Tacotti and Count Karowsky cross themselves, leaving a cemetery. Both Catholic—the Baron being Italian and the Count being Polish, or so I believed at the time— they were prone to do that, so I thought nothing of it at the time." My comment got a few chuckles from the more staunch members of the Church of England at the table. "But while I took little notice of the event, I remember being struck by how alike the two men looked, like a mirror image of each other. And the impression stayed with me.

"It wasn't until we were driving by the same cemetery, after Lady Morton had rescued me, that the memory came back to me. And that was when I realized the mirror image I had seen was of the two men crossing themselves. I remembered hearing, or reading, at one point or another, that Russians, members of the Russian Orthodox Church, cross themselves from right to left. Catholics, and Anglicans, touch the left shoulder first and then the right. But Russians cross by touching their right shoulder first, and then the left." I could see that several guests at the table were visualizing the gesture in their mind.

"I needed to confirm my hunch, so I asked the concierge for the closest Russian Orthodox Church. I preferred not to go to one in Nice, in case I was observed, so he recommended one in Menton. This morning, I drove to the Russian church in Menton, and confirmed that Russians make the sign of the cross in the same way Count Karowsky had done. So I concluded that Count Karowsky was not Polish, but was in fact Russian."

"Bravo!" Uncle Albert exclaimed, and clapped enthusiastically. A few dinner guests joined in with a little more restraint.

Dinner continued with a cheerful exchange of questions, affirmations by Lady Morton that she had always suspected Count Karowsky's duplicity, and much wine.

As the party disbanded for drinks and coffee, I made my way to the verandah. A gentle breeze blew in from the Mediterranean and I could hear the waves lapping gently in the darkness. The moon shone bright and clear, illuminating the white flowers in the garden below like thousands of little stars.

I heard someone approaching, and by the way he walked, I knew it was James. He leaned on the balustrade beside me. For a moment, I recalled our meeting at the casino.

But things had changed since then, I could feel it. I could not put my finger on why, but his attitude towards me this evening had shifted.

"How are you, Caroline?" he asked.

I turned to look at him as he did the same. In the moonlight, his face appeared as though carved by an Italian master. I wanted to run my fingers over it, to assure myself that he was real.

My eyes lingered on his for a moment—their crystal blue had turned to deepest ink. "I'm fine," I said. "And you?"

I returned my gaze to the impenetrable darkness where the peaceful sea met the night sky.

"I'm well," he answered. "I only wish it were me who'd come to your rescue in the garden," he said in a low voice.

I held my breath for a moment.

"I have a secret I would like to tell you," I said, my soft voice barely audible above the noise spilling out of the dining room.

He did not reply, but I could feel his eyes searching my face. I hesitated, wondering which one of my two secrets to share with him.

I turned to face him. "I know where the flower is," I said, as gently as a lover. And a smile spread across my face.

James' laugh burst out into the night, as though he had been holding his breath as well.

"Don't let go," I yelled.

"I won't," yelled James down to me.

He was holding me by the ankles the next day as I leaned over the precipice of a cliff. Perhaps it was not the brightest way to get at the milky orchid.

Stretching my fingers towards its freshly opened blossoms, I felt like Achilles being dipped in the river Styx, and hoped my heel would not slip out of James' hand and be my undoing.

"Got it," I said, and I felt James pull me up in the most ungentlemanly fashion.

Once back at the top, he helped me up, and we stood there, facing each other, gazing at the tiny flower nestled in my hands.

With The Golden Platypus firmly in Uncle Albert's grip, and the hopes of the rest of the Royal Society dashed for another year, the ship of fools had set its sights on the unsuspecting residents of the shores of Lake Garda, Italy.

I agonized over the decision of whether to go to Italy with my uncle or give up my position as his secretary. I didn't think being a secretary was for me, or at least not in the manner required by my uncle. Perhaps there was another penniless fourth son of an Earl who could fill my spot.

Staying on with Poppy on the Riviera for a few more months to help her search for a new architect and a villa, and joining a few fabulous American parties, was much more my speed.

Perhaps I also needed some distance from James. But I didn't linger on that thought.

My uncle tried to induce me to remain in his employment with promises of midnight parties and exotic blooms, but I'd had enough of flowers for a while.

In the end, it was Lady Morton who helped me decide.

"Oh, Lady Caroline," she gushed, leaning towards me over her *terrine de canard truffe* during dinner that night. "My Cecil has managed to take a few days off from the bank. He's coming down on The Blue Train tomorrow. Isn't it wonderful?"

I racked my brain for the most appropriate answer. What would get me the furthest away from Cote d'Azur, the fastest? And unfortunately, I saw only one escape route still open to me—Lake Garda.

I ran up to my uncle's suite.

"Hello, Wilford," I greeted my uncle's man as he opened the door. "Is my uncle about?" I asked as I scanned the empty room.

"No, My Lady. As it is his final night in Nice, and as the pain in his toe has subsided to some degree, he has joined the rest of the gentlemen of the Royal Society at Chez Gustave's for dinner. I believe your uncle was looking forward to taking well-deserved pleasure in gloating about the prize currently in his possession."

"Oh," I said, crestfallen. I had hoped to inform my uncle of my reconsideration, so arrangements could be made for me for the boat and then the train to Lake Garda. I knew the party was departing early the next morning. Time was running out.

"If I may, Lady Caroline," Wilford interrupted my thoughts, "I have taken the liberty of securing a passage for you on tomorrow's trip to Lake Garda."

I looked up at the valet in dismay. "How did you know?" I asked, incredulous.

"I chanced upon Lady Morton's maid this afternoon, who informed me of the impending arrival of Lady Morton's son, Cecil. I took the liberty of instructing the hotel's maid to pack your trunks for early departure tomorrow. I hope I have not misjudged the situation," he said with a slight bow.

"Not at all, Wilford," I said, beaming at him. "Not at all."

Early the next morning, M. Francois stood in his patent leather shoes on the top step of Hotel Paradis. He was alternately waving his monogrammed handkerchief in farewell and dabbing at wayward tears in the corners of his eyes. I wondered whether he was shedding tears of sorrow due to the departure of the members of the Royal Society for Natural History Appreciation and their Golden Platypus, or whether these were tears of joy over the recompense I had handed him this morning.

Either way, I was sure M. Francois was sorry to see us go.

THE END

Thank you for reading *Murder at the Grand Hotel*, Book 1 in the Lady Caroline Murder Mysteries series. The adventures continue in Book 2, *Death in the Garden* on Lake Garda in Italy.

Visit https://isabellabassett.com if you would like to read the Historical Notes for this book, get in touch with me, learn more about this and other mystery series I write, or to read about beautiful Switzerland, where I live.

MORE BOOKS BY ISABELLA BASSETT:

The Old Bookstore Mysteries series about an old Swiss bookstore with a peculiar black cat.

Book 1: Out of Print

Book 2: Murderous Misprint

Book 3: Suspicious Small Print

Book 4: Reckless Reprint

Book 5: Incriminating Imprint

Book 6: Scandalous Snow Print

Book 7: Blackmail Blueprint

Printed in Great Britain
by Amazon